I0725667

A Marriage Of Convenience

BY

STEVIE TURNER

Copyright

© Stevie Turner 2018
All rights reserved

All characters and names of characters are fictitious and a product of the author's imagination. Any similarity to persons living or deceased is purely coincidental. No part of this book may be reproduced in any written, electronic, recording, or photocopied form without written permission of the author. The exception would be in the case of brief quotations embodied in critical articles and reviews, and pages where permission is specifically granted by the author Stevie Turner.

Contents

Blurb

Gerrie Hermann, aspiring rock star from a rich South African family, has an unusual proposal for Sophie Woods when he meets her for the first time in their university canteen.

Strait-laced Sophie has never done anything out of the ordinary in the whole of her 19 years.

When she decides to take Gerrie up on his offer she has no idea that her decision is going to affect the rest of her life in ways that she could never have foreseen, even in her wildest dreams.

Acknowledgements

My thanks go to Maria Lazarou at Obsessed by Books Designs for the cover and for formatting the manuscript.

x

Part One – March 1997

Chapter One

"I hear on the grapevine you're seeking a quick way to pay off your debts."

I glance up as a stocky young guy with clean-looking brown hair falling to his waist puts his lunch tray down opposite me and takes a seat. I don't know him but have often seen him around the campus carrying a guitar in a case on his back. I don't think he stays in Halls, so I come to the conclusion he must be one or two years older than me.

"I might be; as long as it's legal and I get to keep my clothes on."

I nibble on my sandwich as nonchalantly as I can, enjoying his throaty chuckle at my remark.

"Well, it'll definitely be legal, but it's up to you about the clothes."

Intrigued, I study his face for more clues. There are two laughing blue eyes trying to hide behind copious amounts of dark facial fuzz, which I swiftly decide he'd look better without.

"Out with it then; I've a lecture starting in twenty minutes."

"Sure." He nods. "It's like this. I'm here on a student visa which runs out at the end of June next year, but it'd be better for my musical career if I can stay in the UK." He takes a bite of his burger and scans my face intently. "So … you agree to marry me, and I put thirty thousand smackeroos in your bank account."

"Bloody hell!" I nearly choke on my food. "You move right along, don't you?"

"Don't give me an answer now. Think about it." He waggles his finger at me. "I'm not saying all this just to get into your pants, I really need to stay here. Things are happening for me and my band."

"Jeez." I look at him aghast. "Married? I don't even know your name!"

"Ha! It's Gerrie Hermann. So you're interested then? What's *your* name, by the way?"

His accent is appealing, but I can't quite place it. I have a terrible mental image of taking him up North to meet Mum and Dad, the straightest, poorest, but proudest parents in all the land.

"Sophie Woods, but I can't see it working." I shake my head.

"Sure it will. You don't have to love me or anything, 'cos I'm basically an arsehole." His eyes twinkle. "We get married, then I go my way and you go yours. Only now you're thirty thousand pounds richer, and I don't have to go back to Gaborone and face dear Papa."

I try not to laugh as I finish up my cola and look at his frayed denim waistcoat and dirty-white tee shirt.

"And where are *you*, arsehole extraordinaire, going to get thirty thousand quid from?"

"I've already got it and more from my parents and from playing gigs. Come with me to the hole in the wall and I'll print you out a balance."

"I've got a lecture in a minute, but I'll think about it."

I must look gullible or desperate for money, but then again,
I suppose I'm both. Gerrie finds me again the next day in the
cafeteria. I notice with distaste the same off –white tee shirt, but
this time without the waistcoat.

"See you at the cash machine at half past four." He winks as
he walks past me. "Don't be late."

The effrontery of the guy is amazing. However, intrigued, I
find myself walking a circuitous route to the accommodation
unit after my lectures end, just to see if he's there. He is; waiting
there looking like Winnie the Pooh on steroids, with a smile on
his face the size of the Blackwall Tunnel.

"I knew you'd come!" He's almost jumping up and down
with glee. "You're not seeing my pin number, but you can have
the print-out."

I look away as he pops his card in the reader and enters the
pin. I still cannot believe somebody who looks the way he does
could possess thousands of pounds in his bank account. He
requests a balance and gives me another grin.

"Mum and Dad are minted. Why do you think I've been able
to get a student visa?"

I take the balance print-out from him, and am surprised to
discover there is over fifty thousand pounds in his account.

"Because you murdered them and stole all their money?" I
look again at the piece of paper just to make sure.

"Tempting, but wrong. I told you, they're wealthy. What do you say? Come down to the bank with me tomorrow lunchtime, and I'll transfer all that lovely money over to your account."

It was all moving too fast. I envisage a summer of not having to work at menial jobs in order to pay Mum and Dad back, who had re-mortgaged their home in order to be able to send me to University. I can repay my debt to them in dribs and drabs so as not to cause suspicion, and be done with it. They'll never find out I am already married, and I can always say to a future partner that I don't need a marriage certificate to prove my commitment. I decide for once in my nineteen years to throw caution to the wind and live dangerously.

"Okay, but wait until exams are over. I'll do the preparations and book it for some time in July, but you'll have to shave though. I hate beards."

Gerrie shakes his head.

"No way. Love me, love my beard."

"I don't love you, and I'm not marrying a guy whose face is full of fuzz."

"Bugger." Laughs Gerrie. "You drive a hard bargain, don't you?"

"Take it or leave it." I reply.

We're now drawn together as though there's an invisible thread running through the pair of us. I begin spending all my breaks and lunchtimes with Gerrie, where we sit and eat cross-legged on the grass outside Halls and he plays me tunes on his guitar. Quite often we're joined by other students. Gerrie can play any tune they name, and we sit there and sing like scouts around a camp fire. I'd rather be with Gerrie all day than attend lectures, but with exams looming we have to do our share of studying too.

As yet I haven't invited him back to my room, and he hasn't asked. Sex doesn't seem to be part of the deal, and anyway, I couldn't envisage kissing him with all that facial hair in the way. Sometimes I catch him looking at me. He has a twinkle in his eye, and I know that if I mention sex then he probably wouldn't decline my offer. However, I'm not that sort of girl who could just come out and say *'how about it then?'* I blame my modesty on my prim and proper parents.

I sometimes find myself wondering whether I'm doing the right thing or have totally flipped my lid. It seems incredible that boring Sophie Woods who has never done anything in life on the spur of the moment is now going to be marrying a virtual stranger without ever giving it much thought at all other than the large amount of money involved. I do not have many close friends at Uni to talk over the situation with. Gerrie seems one of those totally laid-back types who doesn't really worry about anything at all and lives in the present. I suppose it's the right way to be, but I tend to weigh up both sides before taking the plunge and making a decision. It must have been his innate charm that has sealed my fate from the beginning.

Typical of Gerrie's laissez-faire style, he's left it to me to organise the wedding. It's not too difficult to sort out seeing as we want to keep it a secret with only the two of us and a couple of witnesses attending. I buy a cheap sundress and matching sandals for the big day, try, and make my grey eyes look alluring with some eyeshadow and mascara, and ask a hairdresser to put some blonde highlights in my shoulder length mousey brown hair. Gerrie has to wait for that all-important marriage certificate before he can apply for his ILR (indefinite leave to remain) status which will eventually lead to British citizenship. He's already lived in the UK for two years while he's been at Uni, so it all looks good for him (and for me come to that).

It's a lovely day for a wedding. Thirty thousand pounds richer, I stand on the steps of Walthamstow Registry Office in the summer sunshine with my new husband of just ten minutes. We thank our two witnesses, and ask them to take some photos of us with my Polaroid camera. The witnesses comply, and then disappear into the throng of passers-by from whence they came. Gerrie looks at me and gives a whoop of joy.

"Yes! Cheers for this Sophie, you don't know what it means to me. The music scene's here in London, and now I can apply for the ILR and follow my dream. I don't know how long it'll take, but at least now I'll have the chance."

"You're welcome, and thanks so much for the money." I laugh with that exhilarated debt-free feeling. "Let's go and celebrate!"

As we walk along The Blackhorse Road to a nearby pub, I take a swift glance at the newly-shaven Gerrie, now sporting a Kirk Douglas-like dimple on his chin, who actually looks devastatingly handsome in a three-piece suit and cravat, with his hair slicked back into a ponytail. He catches my eye and puts a casual arm around my shoulder.

"So, you like the new me, eh?"

"Sure." I blush furiously. "You've scrubbed up pretty well."

"You're not so bad yourself." His gaze travels up and down my body in an instant. "Fancy coming along to my gig tonight at The Standard? We can go for a curry afterwards if you like?"

I'm suddenly happy that we're not going our separate ways straight off, and enjoy feel of Gerrie's arm about me and the obvious agreeable effect that I'm having on him. I turn my head to look in his direction and ask the question that's been buzzing around my head for ages.

"So why didn't you just apply for British citizenship like everybody else?"

"Ha!" He throws back his head in a roar of laughter. "I did a few months back, but apparently I'm not of good moral character."

"Really?" I shake my head. "Why's that?"

Gerrie shrugs.

"Oh, probably because I've got long hair, play in a band, and study Music instead of Engineering. Here we are." He opens the pub door and waves me through first. "What'll you have?"

I detect a pleasant aroma of aftershave as I brush past him.

"Just cola please."

"What my wife wants, she shall have." Gerrie walks up to the bar and signals to the landlord. "Grab a table. I'll be back in a minute."

I still cannot believe I'm married; it seems like it's all happening to somebody else. I watch Gerrie chatting to the barman before looking down at the plain gold band now adorning the third finger of my left hand. Of course I know it's only a marriage of convenience, but there's a buzz from knowing that thirty thousand pounds is now sitting in my bank account just waiting to be spent.

Gerrie struts towards me, head held high and carrying a frothy pint of beer with my cola. He slaps both glasses on the table, sits down, and gives me a wink."

"So… wife of mine. Tell me a little bit more about yourself."

This is madness! A mental picture of Mum and Dad meeting Gerrie flashes through my mind.

"I'm in the first year of studying Psychology, as you probably know by now. I've always wanted to be a social worker." I take a sip of cola and try not to drown in those baby blue eyes. "I still live in Halls. My parents live a few miles from Manchester. I'm an only child. How about you?"

"Not much to tell really." He gives another shrug. "I'm twenty. Mum and Dad pay the rent on a small flat for me near the station - they live in Gaborone. I'm the youngest of three. I'm gonna be a rock star."

I have no idea where Gaborone is, and so decide to hide my ignorance and look it up later on Google. Gerrie states his last few words with the utmost sincerity, and I believe him. As far as I'm concerned, there's no doubt he already looks like a cross between younger versions of James LaBrie from *Dream Theater*, coupled with a touch of the top-hatted 'Slash' from Guns 'n' Roses.

"Why did you pick *me*?"

I make a pleasant study of his features while he thinks up an answer.

"Well… I've asked most of the girls on campus, but you're the only one who has said *yes*."

I cannot help but laugh.

"So you weren't attracted to my stunning good looks and exuberant personality then?"

He has the grace to appear embarrassed.

"Err…"

"Don't worry." I wave away the awkwardness. "It's just a business arrangement. I'll be off just as soon as I've watched you play your gig."

I feel a slight twinge of disappointment at the thought.

Chapter Two

I suppose some of my contemporaries would call me *strait-laced.* Certainly the people I'm sitting with in The Standard music venue might do just that as soon as my back is turned. They eye me suspiciously as I sip a cola. A wild-looking redheaded girl, pale and with pre-Raphelite curls, looks me up and down as Gerrie sound-checks with his band and plays power chords on the stage in front of us.

"Are you Gerrie's girlfriend?"

I shake my head and answer truthfully.

"No."

I see her gaze stray to my left hand, and I can tell she's desperate for a more detailed explanation. I could kick myself for forgetting to take the bloody ring off.

"You're at the university?" She shouts as the band warm up.

"Yeah." I nod. "Psychology, first year."

"I'm Maxine. I don't study at the university, but I work there in the clearing office." The girl then gestures to a guy next to her that I've seen around the campus. "He's Olly."

"Hey." Olly nods in my direction. "Where did Gerrie find *you*?"

The *you* comes over as slightly condescending. I dislike him immediately and reply in the same off-hand manner.

"By the campus cash dispenser. I was looking for thirty thousand pounds."

Olly yawns and turns away from me towards the stage.

"Aren't we all, darling?"

I decline to inform him that I found just what I was looking for, and that I am not his darling. Instead, I concentrate on my new husband, twiddling the knobs on his amplifier and now decked out in black leather trousers, scuffed cowboy boots, and a rather fetching black tee shirt boasting the logo *'If you don't want oral sex, keep your mouth shut'*. His brown hair is long and free, and in the spotlight it falls in shining waves down his back. Stubble is already growing back on his chin. I find myself wanting to eat him alive.

The band plays loud heavy metal, to the delight of the assembled crowd. I recognise a few covers, but mostly I think they're playing their own material. The singer, suitably hirsute but thinner than Gerrie and not as tall, growls in a kind of creature-of-the-deep way. He's wearing about fifteen tee-shirts emblazoned with the band's name *Thrash,* and as he sings he removes them and throws them out into the audience. Gerrie struts about the stage with his guitar. I don't really like the music, and all I can think of when I see the band's name is the affliction *thrush*, which luckily so far my dubious alter ego of *Miss Frigidaire* and I have managed to avoid.

Halfway through the band's set there's a break. Olly's already got the drinks in. Gerrie bounds over to our table, sits down next to me, and takes a deep swig of beer, indicating with a forefinger towards the singer who has manoeuvred himself next to Maxine.

"This is Ace, a good friend of mine."

"Hi Ace." I flash my best smile. "Great first set."

"Cheers." Ace lifts his pint of beer. "Over there next to Olly are Dave and Stu."

I look over to where two identical twins are standing together and lifting pints in unison.

"Hi guys." I'm mesmerised by their similarity. "Two peas in a pod."

"Yeah, that's us." Dave laughs. "Except that Stu can't play the drums and I can't play bass guitar."

Maxine and Ace kiss, and I look away embarrassed. Gerrie puts his arm around me and hisses hot breath in my ear.

"How about a curry later on and then back to my flat after we've helped Stu load up the van? It's our wedding night, after all!"

It's Sunday tomorrow; exams are over and there's no more coursework. I think it's time to finally address a very important issue before I call Dad to come and pick me up for the summer holidays. I've been on the pill for long enough; it's just that now I'm stuck with the *Miss Frigidaire* label I've found out pretty quickly there are very few guys remotely interested in helping me lose my cumbersome virginity, and the ones that try their luck I wouldn't touch with somebody else's barge pole, let alone mine.

"Okay." I shiver with anticipation. "Fine with me."

The curry is steamingly hot, making my eyes water and my

mouth tingle. I feel as though I don't fit in with this group, who are all older than I am and as far as I can tell have seen it all and done it all. I've done zilch with my life thus far, and it shows.

We each pay our share of the bill, and feeling as though I couldn't eat even another poppadum I enjoy the walk back along the Blackhorse Road to Gerrie's flat. He carries his guitar case in one hand but has his other arm around my shoulders. The traffic is still heavy even though it's nearly midnight, and car horns honk for their owners' right to rule the road. London is alive, Gerrie's body heat is pulsing through my body, and I'm young and eager to sample what so far I've been missing.

The flat is the upstairs part of what looks like a Victorian terraced house. Lights are on in the downstairs windows.

"Ash and Charlie are still up." Gerrie unlocks the front door and we enter the communal lobby. "They're great guys – I'll introduce you to them tomorrow."

He then opens his own front door and I follow him up a flight of carpeted stairs to what I soon determine is a small 4-room somewhat untidy flat.

"I'm going to take a shower." Gerrie places his guitar case down carefully on the landing. "You can come in with me if you want."

I try to hide how aghast and turned on I am all at the same time after receiving this invitation. My heart begins to race.

"I bet you say that to all the girls."

"Yeah, I do." He gives me a mysterious smile. "So what d'you say?"

The picture of a ripe cherry waiting to be picked comes to mind. It's time for me to sample the fruit.

"Okay." My voice sounds breathy. "Now?"

He's already divesting himself of his clothes as he makes his way to the bathroom.

"No time like the present."

I follow the curve of his buttocks with hungry eyes. He turns to face me as I undress shyly. I have never seen an erect penis before. I touch it briefly as we step into the shower, and there is an answering twitch.

"It doesn't bite." Gerrie turns on the tap and water cascades over us. "Not unless you want it to."

I'm reassured but mesmerised by his manhood. He dabs shower gel onto his hands and soaps my breasts. The sensation causes me to move closer to him, and we kiss. I wrap my arms around his neck.

"Are all men just life support machines for their penises?"

"I reckon." Gerrie exhales softly, sinking his head into my shoulder.

I feel his own throbbing desire against my abdomen, and somehow know for certain that beneath his rather macho exterior my husband is a gentleman, and that nothing will happen to me that I do not wish.

Chapter Three

I'm awake with a rather sick feeling inside. I prop myself

up on one elbow and glance at the digital clock over on Gerrie's side. *Three thirty five.* Waves of nausea and undigested curry wash over me. I wish I'd never eaten something I would not normally have even contemplated.

Moonlight shines in through thin curtains, allowing me to find my way to the bathroom, where I thankfully empty my stomach. I sit weakly on the toilet and purge my bowels over and over again.

Gerrie does not appear. It's another two hours before I can climb back into bed beside him, having had another quick un-erotic shower. I fall asleep immediately and wake to bright sunshine, feeling much improved. I am alone, but can hear the muted sound of a radio from the direction of the kitchen.

I am naked; my clothes are still in the bathroom where I left them. I climb out of bed and put on Gerrie's dressing gown which is hanging behind the door. As I cross the landing to the kitchen I see him standing by the kettle in his pants, eating toast.

"'Morning sleeping beauty." He winks at me. "Want some tea?"

"Yes please." I nod. "Sorry if I woke you last night. I threw up in your bathroom."

"Oh?" He gives me a quizzical look. "I didn't hear a thing. Feel alright now?"

"Yes, and hungry too."

He puts his arms around me and my head rests agreeably on his chest.

"Tea and toast coming up." He cups my chin with his hands so that I'm staring into his eyes. "Look…I didn't realise it was your first time last night. If I did, I'd have made you coffee first."

I can't resist a chuckle, and pull my face into a grimace.

"It's okay. I just hope I came up to your expectations."

"Course you did, but we've got all summer to practise even more." Gerrie's hands caress my buttocks. "I didn't think I'd like you so much."

He kisses me and my brain shifts into fifth gear.

"My parents are expecting me home for the summer, but I don't want to go now."

"Then don't." Gerrie turns away to pop some bread into the toaster. "I've got a double bed, as you found out. Stay here with me – don't worry about finding digs for your second year. It'll be great to have some company."

I wrack my brain to find a suitable solution to the problem.

"What the hell do I tell them?"

He performs a rather suggestive pelvic thrust.

"Say you've just got married and you're having too much raunchy sex to even think of going home."

I sigh.

"I'll have to tell them I've met someone and want to stay in London, but will go home for a couple of weeks before the new term begins."

"Sure." He nods as he switches the kettle on. "I've never got on too well with my parents, but they're keeping me in relative luxury so I phone them every week or so. I can't wait to see their faces when I tell them I've got a wife!"

I cannot hold my curiosity in check any longer.

"What do they do for a living?"

There, I've said it. There's a bit of a silence while Gerrie pours out some tea and spreads butter on two slices of toast, but as he hands my breakfast to me I'm relieved that he replies to my question.

"Dad's a diamond merchant, and he also owns one of the companies where the diamonds are graded. He was lucky twenty years' ago to have my grandfather's money behind him and be in the right place at the right time."

"Wow." I'm impressed and cannot hide it. "No wonder you have thousands in your bank."

He waves away my reply and rolls his eyes.

"Yeah, I expect he'll be generous up to the point where I call and say I'm not coming home. He decided to humour me for a couple of years and let me travel to the UK, but Dad's a control freak. He wants me to learn the business and the value of money and sit there grading diamonds all day. I'd rather top myself. My brother is jumping at the chance to take over the business, so let him get on with it."

He looks momentarily rather sad. I bite off a chunk of toast and say that thing that must be said.

"They'll think I'm a gold-digger, but hey, you came to me, remember? My parents don't own a brass farthing, and they took out a second mortgage so that I could go to Uni. I did plan to pay them back when I get a decent job after graduation, but now I can do it straight away. I don't expect you to give me any more money - I want to make that clear right away."

Gerrie flops down into a seat at the kitchen table and yawns.

"If you like we can go back to bed and get to know each other further, but then I'm going to give the parentals a call and introduce you. Dad will be furious that I've disobeyed him. Mum's hidden her own opinions for years, but I'm sure she'll love you. Don't worry about taking my money, as Dad will stop paying any more into my bank account as soon as he realises I'm not coming home. We'll have to work maybe evenings and weekends to pay the rent and be able to eat, but at least I'll be gigging and doing something I love. Of course you still have the choice to walk away from it all and carry on as before, 'cos after all, that *was* the original plan."

I sit opposite him and finish my tea.

"Do I get a say in the going back to bed bit?" I chew the last piece of toast and try not to grin. "Can we go *now*?"

Gerrie laughs as he gets to his feet, picks me up, and then carries me off to the bedroom.   This time I'm not so terrified. We take our time, and as I climax for the first time I realise why the corridors of Halls are so busy every night.

I hope I look smart enough. My mouth is dry with nerves as Gerrie picks up the landline extension phone by the bed and dials his parents' number. I will soon be speaking to my new in-laws, who doubtless will hate every bone in my body.

He has shown me a photo of his parents; his father an older, shorter-haired version of himself. His mother had obviously been quite stunning as a younger woman, with blonde hair and peachy skin still lustrous in middle age. We sit side by side on the pristine bed which had recently seen us writhing around in ecstasy. Gerrie immediately begins to speak in what I assume is Afrikaans, and then switches to English.

"Dad, I'm speaking English, because I want to introduce you to Sophie. Sophie, meet my father Brett."

He passes me the receiver and I imagine Gerrie senior in my mind.

"Hi." I croak.

"Hello." The voice is deep and authoritative. "How are you?"

"Okay thanks."

I'm a bit lost for words, and Gerrie snatches back the receiver.

"Is Mum there?"

His tone softens as he converses with his mother in Afrikaans before switching to English.

"Mum." Gerrie sounds as nervous as I feel. "Sophie is my wife. We were married recently." He hands me the receiver. "Sophie, have a word with my mum, Eila."

Eila and I have any chance to talk cut short, because I can hear Brett Hermann launch into a tirade of Afrikaans down the line. I need no instruction in the language to realise that my father-in-law is obviously deeply, deeply pissed off.

Gerrie ends the call in mid-rant.

"Well, that's the end of that."

He flops back onto the duvet, exhaling forcefully. I lie down close to him and give him a cuddle.

"You've got to earn your living now?"

"Yep." He laughs. "I'm free as a bird, but unfortunately there'll be no more money in my bank account unless I put it in there myself."

"We'll get jobs, don't worry." I kiss the side of his face. "This is all my fault. I'll wait at tables every evening if I have to, or even clean toilets. Maybe your dad will even come around in time?"

"No chance, and no, it's not your fault." Gerrie shakes his head. "The bastard's enjoying this. He'll see me rot in hell first."

I stroke his cheek with one finger.

"We'll get by, don't worry. When I've paid Mum and Dad back, there'll still be quite a few thousand left over."

"And I've still got enough to live on for a while." Gerrie rolls himself on top of me. "We'll make it last. Stu's got seven gigs for *Thrash* coming up, and I can always teach guitar."

We kiss passionately and I am reassured, although secretly disappointed that the endless supply of money will soon be gone.

Chapter Four

We have six weeks of summer in front of us, and we're in love. Yes, mousey old Sophie has found her soul mate in the most serendipitous way. I would never have given Gerrie a second glance if I'd passed him in the street, and I thank my lucky stars each day that fate has brought us together.

I find temporary work stacking shelves in our local supermarket. Gerrie plays gigs with his band and advertises his services as a guitar tutor. Soon we have a steady stream of small boys clutching oversize Stratocasters climbing up the stairs to our front room, while their mothers wait outside in gas-guzzling Chelsea tractors and look forward to the day when their sons will be able to buy them marbled mansions in Knightsbridge with accompanying triple garages for the Rolls Royce's, Bentleys and Aston Martins.

Gerrie likes cooking more than I do, and we take it in turns rustling up something edible each evening. I take full advantage of the discount on our shopping bill that I'm entitled to by working at the supermarket, and as August turns into September I'm proud that we're getting along fine without any injection of cash from Brett Hermann. Only one thing is bothering me; the period that usually arrives when I stop taking the pill for a week doesn't seem to be happening.

I bring up the subject when we're lying in bed, sated with sex and with my head on Gerrie's chest.

"I think I need to go to the doctor's."

There's a brief silence while this information is digested. Gerrie lifts himself up on one elbow to look at me.

"Why?"

"I haven't had a period since early July, and my breasts are really sore."

"So?" Gerrie shrugs. "Periods are often late, aren't they?"

"Not since I've been taking the pill." I sigh. "I think I may be pregnant. Remember the first time we had sex and I threw up? I remember now being told how an upset stomach can interfere with the pill's efficiency."

"Oh God!" Gerrie flops back on the pillows. "That's all we need! You'll have to get rid of it. There's no way I'm ready to be a father."

I'm aghast at his reply. Killing our child before it was even born had never entered my head.

"There's no way I could ever have an abortion." I sit up and look across at him. "I like to be able to sleep at night with a clear conscience."

"Well, let's just see what the doctor says, eh?"

He turns over on his side, away from me. I'm hurt and frankly disgusted at his reaction.

"**Mrs** Hermann, the urine test and my examination does indeed confirm that you are in the early stages of pregnancy."

I'm stunned. I'm not sure what to say. I sit there in a kind of stupor, taking pamphlets and paperwork from the doctor's hand without really listening to the words coming out of his mouth. All I can think about is what my parents are going to say. Their home is re-mortgaged but my burgeoning career as a social worker is over before it's even started. How can I face them or go back to University in the autumn with a big belly or even worse later on, haggard and worn out with a screaming baby on my hip?

"Mrs Hermann, are you happy about the pregnancy?"

The tears streaming down my face must have given the game away. I nod blindly and stand up.

"Oh, yes. Absolutely."

I am only nineteen, but my life is racing away from me, out of control. My parents do not even know I am married, let alone pregnant. Their good, biddable daughter has gone *bad*. I bite the inside of my mouth just to wake myself up in case it's all been a terrible nightmare, but I find to my dismay that the pain confirms I am not asleep.

"On your way out, make another appointment at the desk for your first check up with the midwife next month."

I cannot even remember what day it is as I stumble back to the flat. Ash and Charlie are obviously on a late shift when they meet me in the lobby on their way out to the hospital. Ash, ever the nurse, takes my hand.

"Soph! You look terrible! Are you alright?"

"Not really." I burst into floods of tears. "I'm pregnant!"

Charlie unlocks their front door.

"Come in and sit down. You need a strong cup of tea."

"I'm stopping you from going to work." I sob.

"No, we're on nights this week. We've just woken up and were going out to meet some friends for dinner."

Charlie gives me a cuddle on the settee, and then Ash brings in some hot, sweet tea and sits down next to me on the other side, a concerned look on his face.

"What does Gerrie think about it?"

My eyes fill up with water again.

"He doesn't want a baby, and there's no way I can ever have an abortion or give a baby of mine up for adoption. Oh God, this is not what I had planned!"

"Life has a way of kicking you in the balls." Charlie pats my back. "When Ash and I *came out* we lost a lot of friends and family, but it gave us a chance to meet new people whom we know we'll be friends with for life. You'll see, when that baby is here, Gerrie will be a doting father. He just needs to get used to the fact that there'll be three of you instead of two, and don't forget that we'd *love* to babysit!"

I manage a thin smile through my tears.

"You're lovely, the pair of you." I hiccup. "I've got to tell Gerrie when his student goes home. He's up there now teaching, with no idea of what's coming."

"You sit here until he's free." Charlie stands up. "We don't mind. Pull the door to when you leave, and it will lock itself. Don't worry, these things have a way of working out for the best."

I try and look through the doctor's paperwork when they've gone, but the words swim in front of my eyes. Faint strains of a riff from 'Smoke on the Water' filter down from upstairs.

"*It's* confirmed. The baby is due on April the fifth."

I cannot bear to look at him and see the disappointment on his face. I sit defeated on our sofa and gaze down at the threadbare carpet with my arms wrapped around my knees.

"Fuck!" Gerrie sighs and punches the wall. "I don't want this! I've got a career to sort out!"

"And what about *my* career?" I'm suddenly angry at him. "At least you can still go to Uni, teach and play your gigs! I've got to give up all hope of mine!"

Somebody actually worse off than him causes Gerrie to have a modicum of sympathy. He comes over to kneel in front of me.

"Get rid of it! You know it's the only way out of this mess!"

I shake my head.

"For you maybe, but not for me. I would never be able to forgive myself." I stand up, edge past him, and begin to pace the room.

"I think I'll go up to Manchester for a week or so and see my parents. I've got to pay them what I owe and tell them the news. It'll give us time to cool down and think properly. You stay here and carry on with your teaching. I'll call in sick at the supermarket for a week. It's only fair that they should know what's going on."

Gerrie nods and gets to his feet. He looks as browbeaten as I feel.

Chapter Five

Was it really only a few months' ago that I closed this very gate and set off excitedly in Dad's car for University? I walk up the path to my parents' terraced house at Astley Green, knowing that Mum has probably already spotted me from behind the net curtains. Sure enough, the front door is thrown open and Mum's beaming smile lights up my dull day.

"Soph! Why didn't you let us know you were coming up? How did you get here?"

"Hi Mum!" I match her smile with another one that I hope looks genuine. "Train and bus. It was okay."

"Come in, come in! Tell me all about what's been happening to you!" She turns to shout in the direction of the upstairs landing. "Len, we have a visitor!"

I put my bag and suitcase down, give Mum a hug, and hear Dad hurrying down the stairs. Mum still wears the perfume I remember, and the smell of her is comforting.

"Oh Mum." I hate myself for starting to cry. "I've got so much to tell you!"

Dad turns it into a kind of group hug. I suddenly wish I'd never left my safe childhood home.

"Sophie! What's up?" Dad holds me at arm's length and looks questioningly at me. "Have you run out of money?"

I shake my head and instinctively wipe my eyes with the back of my left hand. I so want to save my parents from the misery I'm about to inflict on them.

"Is that a wedding ring?" Mum stares at my hand. "Sophie, are you married?"

They look at me, waiting for an answer. Mum's mouth is open in a little 'o' of surprise. I nod and make my way to the front room and they follow behind like a pair of ducklings. I fling myself down on the settee, which I see still bears my red felt tip marks of another age.

"It was supposed to be just a marriage of convenience so that he could stay in the country. He gave me thirty thousand pounds, so I've come to pay you back – all of it."

"You don't owe us that much, only ten thousand." Dad shakes his head and sits down in his armchair. "Where is he now? Do you live with him?"

Mum cuddles me on the sofa, which makes me want to cry again, but I am determined to get my story out.

"Yes I live with him. It's strange, but we actually fell in love after the wedding. He's South African. His name is Gerrie Hermann."

"Bloody hell!" Dad lets out a long breath. "What does he do for a living?"

"He teaches guitar and plays gigs with his band in-between going to Uni. That's where I met him – in the canteen after a lecture. He's a Music student." I screw up a bit more courage. "But there's something else I have to tell you. I'm pregnant."

There's a terribly long silence while the information is digested. I lean in against Mum, who kisses the top of my head.

"You're not yet twenty. You can do the University course in a few years' time. If you move up here I can babysit. We'll work something out."

Bless her. My tears flow freely with the knowledge that Gerrie will only live in London.

Dad finds his voice at last.

"Was the pregnancy planned?"

"Of course not." I reply in-between sobs. "I was on the pill, but I had a stomach upset."

"What's done is done and it can't be changed." Mum has reverted to her usual no-nonsense self. "We'll support you all we can. Keep the money – you're going to need it."

"No." I shake my head. "I've already written you out a cheque. It's in my bag."

"We won't take it." Dad replies adamantly. "It stays in your bank."

What else can I do but sob? Mum holds me close and I inwardly curse the day that Gerrie Hermann came into my life. However, guilt plagues me later in bed that night, and I decide to write out a cheque for the ten thousand pounds I owe them and leave it on the kitchen table when I go back to London. If they tear the cheque up then that's up to them, but at least I would have eased my conscience.

The same wood pigeon is cooing outside my bedroom window that I'm sure has been there since my early teens. Everything around me is so familiar, yet nothing is the same anymore. The pink duvet cover adorned with red roses covered me as a girl, but now I am a woman, soon to bring another life into this world. I have been so very stupid.

I sit up in bed and look at the clock, which shows 08:45. I pick up my mobile phone from the bedside table, but there's no message from Gerrie. Dad will already be on his way down to the canal to take the first group of tourists on a morning boat ride. Mum rattles around downstairs making drinks.

It's time for me to get up and face what the day can throw at me. I keep waiting to feel sick or faint; isn't that what all pregnant women do? However, apart from sore breasts I feel as fit as a fiddle and desperately hungry. I can hear Mum humming to herself as I pad downstairs and slink into a chair at the kitchen table. She gives me a smile

"Did you sleep okay?"

"Yes thanks." I nod. "It's a relief now I've told you everything."

Mum hands me a cup of steaming coffee.

"Of course it is. We'll stand by you. There's no way I'll see my daughter or grandchild want for anything."

I get up and hug my mother, who is already making me a toasted bacon sandwich. It occurs to me that all the money in the world cannot make up for the love I've received over the years from my two wonderful parents. I am truly lucky.

"Gerrie's father is a diamond merchant out in South Africa, but he doesn't approve of me and won't be giving us a penny."

"You don't need him." Mum grimaces as she hands me a plate of food. "You can come home any time. We'll be pleased to have you and the baby here."

I make short work of my sandwich, and shoo Mum upstairs while I wash up. After an invigorating shower I wrap a towel around me and go back into my bedroom to get dressed. My phone is buzzing away by the bed. I pick it up.

"Hi." Gerrie's accented voice booms down the line. "This is the third time I've rung."

"I was having a wash. How's it going with you?"

There's a brief silence before he carries on.

"I miss you. Are you coming back? Sorry I punched the wall."

He sounds like a little boy who has lost his mother in a crowd, but deep down inside I'm still angry.

"Mum says I can stay here as long as I like. She says she'll babysit if I go to University up here."

I hear a loud *tut* of disapproval.

"So that's it? You'll be living two hundred miles away with our child?"

"You don't want it anyway." I remind him. "Remember?"

"It was a shock, but I'm getting used to it now." He gives a throaty chuckle. "Sorry, Soph. Come home, eh?"

I am home, but then again I'm not. My home is with Gerrie. I come to the realisation that I've made my bed, and now I want to lie in it with my husband. I feel mightily relieved that he hasn't tossed me away like yesterday's fish and chip paper.

"At the end of the week. They haven't seen me for months."

"Okay. Love you."

This is the first time he has actually said those two words that every girl wants to hear. A rush of joy courses through my body.

"Love you too." I reply.

Chapter Six

This baby is making me so bloody tired. I walk around in a fog of fatigue every day, willing my shift at the supermarket to be over. They've kept me on for now and Gerrie has gone back to Uni, but I've given up my Psychology course. What's the point of starting a new term when I know I'll never be able to finish it?

The midwife tells me that I'll feel better once three months have passed, but at the moment all I want to do is go to sleep or *eat, eat, eat.* I've put on a bit of weight because just as soon as I finish my dinner I feel like I could eat another one, and sometimes do.

Ash and Charlie cluck around me like two mother hens when Gerrie's out playing gigs, but I think Gerrie is too focused on becoming a rock star to care too much about the coming baby. *Thrash* are getting quite a following around the clubs and pubs. I know he wants me to go with him and watch them play, but I find I'm ready for bed at half past nine. I'm sure Ace and Maxine think I've turned into some kind of frump, and I've started to believe it myself. What nineteen year old goes to bed before ten like I'm doing now? *A pregnant one, that's who.*

I lie there mulling things over in my head. There have been no more phone calls to Brett and Eila, and as far as I know Gerrie has not told them of my pregnancy. From what he's said in the past, his older brother already has three children, so it's not as though our baby will be their first grandchild. It occurs to me that it might be a good thing to get Eila on my side, if only I could find out her phone number.

Does Gerrie have an address book? I can find out!

I'm suddenly galvanised into action. I look around the flat until I find Gerrie's Filofax in one of his rucksacks, which is crammed full of telephone numbers. I reach over for my mobile phone and type *Eila Hermann* into a new message box together with her number. I sit up in bed with my heart racing, and *Ask Jeeves* the time difference. Gaborone is 2 hours ahead of London, and so it's a distinct possibility that Eila will be fast asleep. Nevertheless, I send her a message confirming that I'm Gerrie's wife and how it was a shame that we didn't get the time to speak to each other previously. I wait a few minutes but there is no response. Disappointed, I put the phone down and fall asleep.

Gerrie wakes me up when he comes in at half past midnight. He's on cloud nine as there had been a talent scout in the audience who had shown an interest in the band. He struts around the room holding his guitar at an uncomfortable-looking angle like a true rock star.

"He wants to see us play again!" Gerrie puts his guitar on a chair and dives on top of me, fully clothed.

"Go and have a shower." I try not to gag. "You're all sweaty!"

He climbs off the bed, somewhat calmer.

"Thanks for your enthusiasm."

"Sorry." I chuckle. "You stink."

I make all the right noises when he eventually shuffles in next to me, but I can hardly keep awake. His social life is definitely interfering with my ability to sleep through the night and be bright eyed and bushy tailed for work the next day. His adrenaline is still pumping and he pushes his groin into my buttocks as I lay there drifting in and out of sleep.

"Come on, I *know* you want it too."

I don't actually but I give in, as it's the only way we're both going to get any sleep tonight.

I'm three months' pregnant and at last the tiredness is starting to wear off. There's not much of a bump to speak of, but I seem to have gained four pounds in weight. The midwife is already clucking her disapproval.

It's Saturday evening, and I've agreed to accompany Gerrie down the road to The Standard tonight, where a talent scout is supposedly going to appear just at the right moment and whisk all the band off to superstardom. I try not to be too censorious, but not too many lucky breaks have been coming our way in recent weeks. I haven't heard back from Eila Hermann, but I've tried not to lose hope.

I take my time getting ready, as I have to compete with the hated Maxine, her of the renaissance curls, wasp waist, and heart-shaped face. I've grown my hair a little bit to sweep down past my shoulders, and allowed the hairdresser to put in a few more blonde streaks. My breasts have increased in size though, and I select a suitable low-cut top. Gerrie whistles his approval.

"Wow! You'll knock 'em all dead tonight." He gives me a kiss. "Shall we tell everyone about the baby? We can't hide it for much longer."

He's right, but I fear the boys and Maxine will know the baby wasn't planned, and will laugh at my stupidity for allowing myself to get pregnant. I nod hesitantly.

"Just as long as you tell them we're married. Then they might think the baby wasn't an accident."

"Who cares what they think?" Gerrie combs his hair into a long ponytail and pats on some aftershave. "They'll all be too busy trying to spot the scout to look at your belly anyway."

I sincerely hope he's right.

At least we don't have to travel in the beaten up old van tonight, as we can walk to the venue. The thought of being hemmed in amongst all those sweaty male bodies is enough to make my stomach turn somersaults.

The pub is packed. Maxine has saved me a seat, and I slide in next to her while the boys unload the van outside. It's a Heavy Metal night, and Metallica's 'One' bursts loudly out of two giant speakers on the stage. Maxine regards me with barely concealed apathy.

"Alright?"

It's now or never. I flash her the most dazzling of smiles.

"Absolutely alright. I'm three months' pregnant."

I've got her interest. She quickly masks an expression of disappointment as she sits up straighter and looks down at my stomach.

"You're shitting me?"

"I got pregnant on our wedding night." I briefly think of chicken curry and intense nausea. "It was very romantic."

"So you and Gerrie *are* married then?" Maxine looks to confirm my wedding ring is still in place. "I asked you whether you were his girlfriend, remember?"

"Yeah." I nod. "But I said no because I was his wife then and now."

"You're throwing your life away." Maxine gloats in that *I'm-glad-I'm-not-pregnant* way and drains her pint of lager. "Bloody hell, it'll be kids having kids."

I want to punch the smug look off her face.

"Better than having them when we're forty." I retaliate. "At least we've got the energy while we're young.

Maxine waves to Ace, who is first in through the door carrying an amplifier.

"Good luck with that then." She holds up her empty glass. "You can't even drink anymore."

I shrug.

"I didn't to start with. Don't worry Maxine, we know what we're doing. We've got it all planned."

I only wish that was true.

I don't really like Heavy Metal music, and Gerrie's guitar is too loud. There's a mosh pit forming by the front of the stage, and I watch the reaction of the audience whilst trying to spot which one might be a talent scout. I start to wonder if the music might be damaging the baby's delicate ears as he or she flips somersaults inside me.

Gerrie is lost in his own little world. I'm not even sure he's remembered that I'm sitting here like a prize prat waiting for him to come offstage. Somebody I recognise from Uni, Pete, sidles up to our table and sits down. He seems happy.

"I haven't seen you for ages!"

"Hi Pete." I shout over the band's noise while keeping one eye on Gerrie. "I dropped out. I'm going to have a baby next April."

"Oh!" Pete looks down towards my abdomen. "Sorry, I didn't know."

It's hard work trying to make my voice heard, and I give up. I flash a smile at him and watch the band. After a short time Pete makes an excuse and shuffles along the bench and wanders off towards the bar. Maxine watches his retreating back.

"See how that one word, *baby,* sends the men running?"

"Only Pete." I sniff. "Gerrie has stayed, and he's more important."

The first half ends but the boys do not come over to us and sit down. Instead they're talking to a twenty-something guy who has stepped up onto the stage. I watch their body language; they're smiling and looking at each other in excitement. I realise that the talent scout must have turned up after all.

Chapter Seven

It's four o'clock in the morning and Gerrie is still writhing from side to side in bed, unable to sleep. I sit up and sigh.

"I'm going to sleep on the settee. This just isn't working."

He shakes his head and climbs out from under the duvet.

"I'll go. Sorry, but it's not every day we get the chance of going on tour to support a big band. It's all starting to happen for us."

"I'm pleased for you." I smile at him and snuggle back under the covers. "Really I am, even though I've been awake all night. What's the tour dates?"

"Probably around the end of Uni. You know… festival time."

"You'll be playing festivals?" I look at him in amazement. "How come the scout picked an unknown band?"

Gerrie shrugs and puts on a dressing gown.

"Probably because the band who were going to support *Death Throes* couldn't come up with the tour bus money, which also has to pay the roadies. I told him I could get it. Just think – Download and Sonisphere and that's just two festivals! We're going to be huge!"

I sit up again.

"How much?"

"Forty thou. I've signed a contract that we'll pay the money by the middle of May." Gerrie gives me a wink. "The boys will pay what they can, but I'll have to talk Dad round."

I remembered the last meeting on Skype.

"You sure?" I ask hesitantly.

"Piece of piss." Gerrie, unsmiling, picks up his guitar off its stand next to his side of the bed. "Go to sleep. See you in the morning."

It's quiet when I wake up and check the time – ten fifteen.

I grab my phone and check the messages, just in case Gerrie's mother has changed her mind.

There's notification of a new message. I read Eila's words with a growing excitement:

'Hi Sophie, sorry I've taken so long to get back to you. I'm pleased to meet you at last. The previous try didn't go down too well! If you like we can have another go?'

I check the message again, but there's no explanation given why she took so long to reply. I quickly send her a message of my own.

'Hi Eila. Yes it will be great to talk to you. I think I'd better tell you though that I'm three months' pregnant, so it's not too much of a shock! Can you call me tonight while Gerrie is out

gigging? It might be better on the landline? Ten o'clock your time?'

Back comes a message that Eila will phone at 8 o'clock my time, and I give a little shiver of anticipation as I climb out of bed. *Should I tell Gerrie?* He might think I'm interfering, so I decide to keep quiet. It will be nice to get to know my new mother-in-law. I've no desire to talk to Brett and it's not my place to mention that Gerrie's band needs forty thousand pounds, but instead I'm looking forward to a nice girly chat across the miles. I'll let Gerrie and Brett talk about money.

I pop my head around the living room door. Gerrie is asleep on the settee, with one arm around his guitar. I can't help smiling at the sight of him. As I take the guitar out from under his arm, he wakes up and grabs it back.

"Hey." He yawns. "See, I did get to sleep eventually."

I laugh.

"So you did. Want some breakfast?"

"Sure." He rubs his eyes. "What have we got?"

"Eggs, bacon, tomatoes and mushrooms? How does that sound?"

"Yeah." He nods approvingly. "I like it."

"Well, we'd better get down to the supermarket then, because until we do, we've only got beans on toast."

"Beans on toast it is then." Gerrie grabs me around the middle with his free arm. "How's my lovely wife?"

"Pregnant and hungry." I pull a face. "There's five slices of bread left. Can I have three?"

"Go on then." He stands up. "You're eating for two now."

At ten to eight the van pulls away with Gerrie inside. I look at the phone and wonder if Eila will call, but right on the dot of 8 o'clock it rings. My heart is beating faster as I pick up the receiver.

"Hello?"

"Hi, it's Eila."

The accent is the same as Gerrie's, and I laugh nervously.

"Were you shocked at my announcement earlier?"

Eila gives a low chuckle.

"You could say that." She nods. "Was the baby planned?"

"Er…not really." I blush furiously. "But we're happy. It's due early April. I'll be having my first scan soon. Hopefully they'll be able to tell whether it's a boy or girl."

"If you're happy and my son is happy, then I can ask for nothing more." Eila smiles into the camera. "How's Gerrie getting on with his band?"

I'm glad to get off the subject of unwanted pregnancies, and Eila has thankfully so far been tactful enough not to ask if the marriage is one of convenience. I assume she already knows the answer to that one.

"Good news about *Thrash*. They'll be supporting *Death Throes*, a big headline band, at the Download and Sonisphere festivals, plus other big venues next summer. They're going on tour as support to *Death Throes* after the term has finished at Uni."

"Well, that's marvellous." Eila's voice sounds approving. "Tell him well done from me."

I decide to give her a little advance warning.

"I think he'll be speaking to you or Brett about it soon. He's very excited."

There is a slight hesitation before Eila replies.

"He's very welcome to call me any time he likes, but I don't think he'll get any joy from his papa."

I'd anticipated her reply. I hesitate before deciding to change the subject.

"How many grandchildren do you have, Eila?"

Her voice softens in an instant.

"Gerrie's brother Raymond has three girls, Amahle, Angel, and Amina. Our daughter isn't yet married, but will soon be."

"What lovely names!" I reply with enthusiasm. "We haven't talked about what to call the baby yet, but I think I'd like something unusual."

"Gerrie's in the right business to learn about strange names for babies." Eila chuckles. As I remember, back in the Sixties Frank Zappa called his children *Moon Unit* and *Dweezil*."

"Moon Unit?" I laugh. "Moon Unit Hermann?"

Eila's laugh is low and throaty, but infectious. I cannot help giggling as well. I like this lady, and take a chance with my next statement.

"Will you tell your husband about the baby?"

At the mention of Brett, I detect a wary tone to her voice.

"He doesn't know we're speaking on the phone. He's angry with Gerrie at the moment, as he had such big plans for his son's future. I'm going to leave it a while until he's in a better mood."

I reluctantly have to agree that to wait would be more sensible. We end the call with promises to keep in touch on a regular basis.

Chapter Eight

Gerrie accompanies me to my first ultrasound scan. I've got a hard little bump now, and I can often feel small fluttering movements inside me. We watch the baby dancing about on a screen as the midwife scans my abdomen with a probe.

"All the measurements are normal, and everything looks as it should. Would you like to know the sex?"

I look at Gerrie and he nods. We are of the same opinion.

"Yes please." I reply with more than a touch of anticipation.

"It's a boy." The midwife smiles. "Definitely male."

I wonder if this result might bring Brett around? Gerrie is obviously thinking along similar lines as he takes the photo of our baby from the midwife.

"Dad will be pleased, I'm sure. He's got three granddaughters so far."

I prop myself up on my elbows while the midwife wipes the gel off my belly.

"Are *you* pleased though?"

"Of course!" He looks down at the photo again. "Every man wants a son, doesn't he?"

Does he? If this is true, then was my dad disappointed when I was born? I make a mental note to ask Mum, and also to send Eila a copy of the scan photo. I'm mightily pleased the baby has all four limbs and is doing what he's supposed to be doing. A boy or a girl would have made no difference to me, but as I get dressed again I have one of those lightbulb moments that I'm sure might go some way in reconciling Gerrie with his father and therefore helping out the band. I pick my moment later on as, stuffed full of pizza and pasta, Gerrie leans back at the table, replete.

"Shall we call the baby Brett? I'm sure your dad would love a grandson named after him. It might bring you two back together."

I watch Gerrie's features carefully for any sign of agreement. He shrugs.

"It's a good idea. It might work, but then again it might not."

I venture a reply.

"No harm in finding out?"

"None at all." He winks at me. "I'll send him a message and let him know, but I'd rather the baby be known as Junior. I don't want to be reminded of that old bastard every day."

"Fair enough." I answer thoughtfully. "Junior's a little bit different."

"It's what many South African sons are called." Brett replies. "But if we're ever invited over there I suppose we'd better use his proper name. Still, I can't see that ever happening, so we don't need to worry about it."

As my pregnancy advances, the pressure on Gerrie increases to come up with the tour money. He's often moody and withdrawn, as Brett isn't answering any phone calls or messages.

"I just want him to realise how big the band could become if we get the chance to support *Death Throes!*"

I sense his frustration as we lie together in bed at the beginning of December. So far we have no idea if his father likes the idea of baby Brett Hermann. Eila is over the moon of course, and at our last conversation lets me know that she is going to speak to Brett about the baby in the near future, and find out if he's actually read any of Gerrie's messages. I think it's something that only a wife will be able to discover.

There's no shortage of budding guitarists traipsing up our stairs at evenings and weekends when Gerrie's not out gigging or doing coursework. At £10 an hour cash-in-hand it's a good little earner for him, and he can make about £200 in one weekend. However, it's far from the £40,000 he needs, and my original nest egg that Gerrie gave me has reduced substantially just living from day to day and buying things for the baby.

I have a spare hour after my supermarket shift before Gerrie returns from Uni. It's his last day there before the Christmas break. I decide to make a quick call to Eila to find out what's been going on. She answers straight away.

"Hi Sophie. How are you?"

"Blooming." I laugh. "There's a definite bump there now."

"Lovely!" Eila chuckles. "How much longer to go?"

"Another four months."

"The last month is the worst." Eila replies. "You can't get comfortable in bed, and the baby feels like it's going to drop out every time you stand up."

"Great. I'm looking forward to that." I sigh. "What does Gerrie's dad think of it all?"

Eila gives a little cough.

"He knows about Brett Junior, because I've told him. He's keeping his opinions to himself, but at least he's not ranting and raving anymore."

"Oh well, that's something anyway." I feel slightly uplifted and decide to stick my neck out and to hell with the consequences. "Gerrie and the band could become millionaires because they've had the offer of a UK month-long tour supporting a major headline band at some big music festivals.

Thousands of people will see them play, and so they have the chance of becoming famous."

"That's wonderful!" Eila's voice sounds genuinely enthusiastic. "Can you tell Gerrie I'm very proud of him?"

"Of course." I reply. "But there's just one thing that's holding them back."

This is crunch time. I wait for my mother-in-law's curiosity to get the better of her.

"Oh?" Eila's interest is plain to hear.

"They need to pay their share of the tour bus fees and the roadies' salaries. Eila…they need forty thousand pounds."

"Good God!" Eila appears stunned. "I'll do what I can, but Brett is the only signatory on the business bank account. He gives me an allowance, but I'd have to save it up for nearly two years to get that amount."

I inwardly curse Eila for being so submissive. I come to the conclusion that she is either afraid of Brett or enjoys the luxury of being kept, but as of yet I'm not sure which.

"We've only got until the middle of May." I try and keep the pleading tone out of my reply. "Do you think your husband would lend us the money and we could pay him back over a period of time?"

"I'll ask him for you."

Her A sounds like an R. It's a strange accent, but I'm getting my ears around it.

"Thanks so much, Eila." I gush. "You don't know what this will mean to Gerrie."

We say our goodbyes and I end the call feeling much happier.

Now comes the moment of truth, as I have to tell Gerrie exactly what his mother is going to do. I pick my moment carefully while we're cuddling in post-coital bliss. I snuggle in closer to his chest.

"I've been doing my bit to help you towards that forty thou."

I sense him looking down at me waiting for an answer, so I carry on regardless.

"Your mum and I have been talking on the phone."

He props himself up on one elbow and stares unsmilingly into my face.

"Sophie, what have you been doing?"

I hate that steely expression of his. I shrug, as though manipulating his mother is a mere bagatelle.

"She's thrilled about the baby. She's going to ask your dad if we can borrow the money and pay him back."

Brett shakes his head.

"He holds all the purse strings. He'll never give in. By playing in a band I've spoiled all his future plans for me, and nobody ever goes against him."

"Well it's about time somebody did." I ease him back down on the pillow and resume our cuddle. "He sounds like a tin pot tyrant to me."

Gerrie puts both hands behind his head and looks up at the ceiling.

"I could have had shitloads of money, any amount I wanted, just as long as I helped to run the business by starting out at the bottom and grading diamonds all day." He exhales a deep sigh. "But I'd rather be dead. Mum does as she's told, but she likes it that way. She'll take Dad's money and then go off to lunch with her cronies. They'll spend two hours moaning about their men, and then go shopping with their generous allowances."

So now I know.

"Let's see what your mum comes up with." I kiss him. "I'll call her in a day or so."

Chapter Nine

Christmas is fast approaching, Uni is over for Gerrie until the New Year, and he has reluctantly agreed to come up North with me and spend a few days with Mum and Dad. Because of the usual patchy public transport on bank holidays, we've arranged to travel on Christmas Eve and return home the day after Boxing Day. I've been decorating the flat, and instead of buying each other presents we're going to save the money to get some of the more expensive baby stuff in the January sales. Mum and Dad are buying us a pram. I've noticed they did take the money out of my bank account after all. It's reduced our savings even more, but I feel relieved that they're not in debt because of me.

I grudgingly spend some more of our precious money on Christmas presents, but decide not to bother writing out cards. Gerrie tells me to buy something for Ace and Maxine, Ash and Charlie, Olly, Dave and Stu. I cannot forget my parents either, who we'll be staying with. As far as I'm concerned this present buying is all a waste of money, but at least I haven't got to buy anything for Gerrie's family.

Just before we leave for Manchester I call Eila.

"Happy Christmas!" I try and sound upbeat. "How are you?"

I can almost see Eila smiling at the other end.

"Busy preparing food for the big day. We've got Raymond, his wife and the girls coming over, but our daughter Skye is going to her fiancée's parents for the holidays."

"Er…did you manage to speak to Gerrie's father regarding the loan?"

Eila hesitates, and my heart beats a little faster.

"I did. Brett's not going for it I'm afraid, but he wants Gerrie to know that if he comes home and takes up the reins in the family business, then he can have all the money he wants."

Bastard!

"I don't think that's going to happen." I say with some force. "We're married now and Gerrie's applied for indefinite leave to stay here. He has his own plans for the future."

"I know." Eila agrees. "But Brett wants him to get a proper job. He says nothing will ever come of trying to get a foothold in the music business."

I try and keep the tears out of my eyes.

"He has a foothold." My voice starts to wobble. "We just need to pay for our share of the tour bus, food and drink, and the drivers' and roadies' salaries."

"Sorry, but I can't help you." Eila sounds genuinely crestfallen. "How's the pregnancy progressing?"

"Very well, but I have to go now. Sorry."

"Okay." Eila replies. "Happy Christmas."

I cannot bear to make any more conversation. I end the call and finish packing.

Gerrie comes to find me. I break the bad news, and we stand there holding each other in abject misery.

$\mathcal{D}ad$ sends me a text to let me know he'll be picking us up from Walkden station. We stand with our luggage on platform 2 at Euston and await the train. Gerrie looks down in the dumps and doesn't even make an effort to speak. He follows me to one of the first class carriages I've splashed out money we can't afford on, and a couple with a baby climb in after us. The baby is fractious, and we move a bit further down the corridor. The screaming wakes up Junior, who has a little kick about.

"That's what we'll have in a few months." I look at him and try to elicit a reaction. However, there is none, and I suspect Christmas is going to be somewhat cheerless this year.

We can still hear the baby giving it his all in the carriage next door. Gerrie, who hasn't said a word since we arrived at the station, stares at me, but it's as though he's looking right through me to somewhere else just out of sight. I'm puzzled, until he grabs my hand, kisses it, and chuckles.

"I've thought of a way to get the old bastard to pay up."

The train starts to move off. I'm pleased it's an express and we're not sitting next to anybody else. I shuffle up closer.

"How?" I ask with genuine interest.

"That screaming baby gave me an idea. We've got to get Ace and Maxine involved though. Ace owes me loads of favours. He'll do it, I'm sure."

"Do what?" I venture.

"Look after Junior for a week or so."

"What!" I swivel around to face him. "You're farming out our baby and he hasn't even been born yet?"

"We've got to make Mum and Dad believe the baby's been kidnapped." Gerrie nods. "We'll tell them the kidnappers are asking forty five thousand pounds for the ransom."

"That's ridiculous!" I shake my head. "You can't do that! You've got to pay by the middle of May? The baby will only be a month old! He'll need to be with me, not bloody Maxine! I won't even be able to breastfeed him!"

Gerrie shrugs.

"So buy formula milk! It'll work though. Mark my words, it'll work. My dad will pay up."

I sit back on the seat and let the rhythm of the train calm my racing thoughts. I am totally opposed to letting Maxine get her hands on Junior, even for a day, and I put my arms around my stomach in a futile attempt to protect him from her. No good will ever come of it I'm sure, but I cannot think of a better way for Gerrie to get the money he needs.

"I don't like it." I mutter. "Maxine won't know what to do with him, and anyway, she'll have to go to work, won't she?"

Gerrie has brightened up no end, and answers my question with ease.

"She can book a week off if we give her enough notice. Don't worry, she won't let any harm come to him, especially if we pay her and she knows she's getting five thousand quid for her trouble."

"I still don't want to do it."

He puts his arm around me.

"It won't be for long. We'll have to get the police involved of course, to make it look genuine. We'll tell them somebody broke into the flat at night and took him."

"I'll see if I can think of something else before then." I give a small shiver. "I just don't like the sound of it."

We do not talk much for the two hours it takes to get to Walkden, as both of us are preoccupied with our own thoughts. I remain determined not to let little Junior out of my sight.

Chapter Ten

Mum has made a real effort. The house is decorated from top to bottom, a large pram-shaped present sits next to the tree, and the dining table groans with every kind of Christmas fare.

They are too polite to be anything other than gracious towards Gerrie, who is still somewhat moody and distant. I know they do not approve of his long hair and 'designer' stubble, but would never mention this fact in our presence. They've let us use their double bed, while they have twin beds in the adjoining room.

Gerrie is a night owl, and rarely goes to bed before midnight. Mum and Dad like to be tucked up by half past ten, with lights out, central heating off, and their old-fashioned clocks wound up ready for the next day. I'm quite happy to stick to their routine, but Gerrie twists and turns in bed, unable to sleep. He cannot strum his guitar because of the noise, and sex is off limits while my parents are laying in the bed next door. He complains bitterly in the darkness, not caring whether I'm awake or asleep.

"I'm going bloody mad here, trying to be the perfect son-in-law."

I sigh and turn over to face him.

"It's only for a few days." I hiss. "Mum and Dad are doing their best. You'll have to put up with it."

"I'm going to take them down to the pub tomorrow and get them absolutely rat-arsed."

I chuckle.

"It's Christmas Day tomorrow. The pubs won't be open in the evening."

"Shit." Gerrie sighs. "*I'm* going to get rat-arsed then. Has your dad got any whisky?"

"You will not!" I whisper. "Behave yourself!"

He pulls me towards him.

"Just a quick one?"

"No! Bugger off, you're getting on my tits!"

"Chance would be fine thing." He turns over and sighs. "Night, night."

I'm glad it's dark and he cannot see me grinning from ear to ear.

"See you in the morning."

Eating a full turkey roast in the middle of the afternoon brings on a kind of soporific stupor around an hour later. The dishwasher rumbles away in the kitchen, and Mum and Dad are out cold in their armchairs. Gerrie sits on the settee half-heartedly watching *The Great Escape* and with his right leg constantly on the go, but I cannot stop yawning.

"Let's go out for a walk." I suggest brightly. "They'll be asleep for ages yet."

"Best idea you've had all day." Gerrie whispers as he jumps up. "What's nearby?"

"We can walk along by the canal. It's nice down there."

"Let's rock!" Gerrie's already out the door into the hallway.

I leave Mum and Dad a little note, grab a set of keys, and put on a warm coat of Mum's. A wave of cold, invigorating air hits us as we walk out of the gate, past the colliery museum towards

The Old Boathouse pub near the bridge, and then down some mossy steps to the canal.

"You can get boat rides along here." I point to where a canal boat is moored up nearby. "The tourists love it."

Gerrie walks on in front until there is room for us to carry on side-by-side. I grab his hand and he gives my fingers a squeeze as he looks down at me.

"Have you thought any more about my plan?"

"I've thought of nothing *but*." I reply. "My parents haven't got that sort of money."

"Well mine *have*." Gerrie's tone is bitter. "I think my way is best, don't you?"

I sigh.

"I can't think of any other way around it."

"We'll go for it then." Gerrie nods. "After Christmas I'll confirm it with Ace and Maxine. Junior won't know what's going on. Just as long as someone's feeding him and wiping his arse, he won't care."

I know my feeble protest is futile, but I like to say what's on my mind.

"*I* care."

"It'll all be over before you know it."

I do hope so. I have what the hippies used to call 'bad vibes' about the whole scenario.

Dad gives me a kiss at the station and hauls the pushchair out of the car's boot.

"Get used to pushing that pram about!"

"Thanks for the present." I hug him. "And thanks for putting us up for three days."

"No trouble at all, and thanks for the slippers." Dad shakes Gerrie's hand. "Pleased to meet you, son. You know you can call us Mum and Dad if you like."

"Cheers." Gerrie cannot hide his surprise. "I'll think about it."

I wave goodbye to Dad and then stand there awkwardly trying to unfold the pram and make it secure.

"I'll never get the hang of this."

Gerrie gives it the once over, and then expertly flips the pram upright.

"My nieces had one almost the same"

I am astounded. We push the empty pram into Walkden station and sit down in the waiting room. I keep imagining Junior inside the pram. I cannot wait for the birth. I lean against Gerrie's arm.

"I hope it wasn't too boring for you, you know, the whole Christmas thing."

Gerrie gives my shoulder a squeeze.

"No, I enjoyed the break. You agreeing to my plan has made me very happy. I promise nothing will go wrong, you'll see."

"What choice have I got?" I shrug. "I know how important this tour is to you."

"It'll make us famous, I *know* it will." He kisses the top of my head. "We'll be millionaires before we're twenty five."

I keep my reservations to myself as we board the train. My husband is on a high, and I for one am not going to be the party pooper who brings him down to earth.

Chapter Eleven

$\mathcal{I}$ hate January. Everywhere seems so dull without any

Christmas lights or decorations, the cold weather is debilitating, and my pregnant abdomen is somewhat distended now. I feel old and ugly compared to the beautiful Maxine, who sits radiant and fragrant on my settee next to Ace as hailstones tap lightly on our window.

"I have to give six weeks' notice of any annual leave." Maxine crosses her legs and looks across at me. "When do you want me to take it?"

"Let's go for the week commencing Monday the twenty fourth of April."

I look up at Gerrie for confirmation.

"Sure." He nods. "We still have three weeks then before the money is due, and by that time the baby will definitely be here."

"Okay." Maxine taps a note into her phone. "And we get five thou, yeah?"

"Of course." Gerrie smiles at her. "We wouldn't expect you to do this for nothing. And Ace, tell Stu not to book any gigs that week, but don't tell him I've got to play a grieving parent."

Ace shrugs.

"What shall I tell him then?"

"Make something up! Tell him I've got galloping knob-rot or something."

I giggle, but have a question of my own.

"Maxine…have you ever made up babies' bottles?"

"All the time." Maxine replies dryly. "I have fifteen screaming children at home."

Ace surprises us all.

"I know how to." He raises a hand. "Mum had her last baby at forty two."

"Bloody hell." I reply. "Poor woman!"

"She loves it." Ace smiles at me. "I've got six younger brothers and sisters."

I like Ace. He's happy-go-lucky. God knows why he's landed himself with Maxine. Another thought comes into my head.

"Where will you stay during that week? Your neighbours will wonder why there's a baby crying."

"My parents have a caravan at Felixstowe." Maxine leans back against Ace and watches me through unfathomable green eyes. "We can stay there. You'll have to bring all the baby stuff down the week before though."

"They can't." Ace shakes his head. "They'll be using it. My mum's done with all her baby things now. I'll get them out of the loft and my sister's old Moses basket when they're not looking. There's loads of baby stuff up there. I'll take some time off work, put everything in the car, and we can have a week's holiday in Felixstowe. It'll be worth it for five thousand quid."

"Will that car make the journey? Where the hell's Felixstowe?" Gerrie looks blank.

Maxine laughs

"It's in Suffolk. It's not too far away. The caravan's a static one on a holiday park near the beach. Nobody will know that baby isn't ours."

"Cheers, the two of you." Gerrie rubs his eyes, relieved. "Thanks very much."

$\mathcal{I}$ slide onto a pub bench next to Maxine and we watch the band setting up. My abdomen nearly touches the edge of the table in front of us now. Junior's awake and kicking, and Maxine looks down at my middle.

"I can see your belly moving. It must feel strange to have a little person inside you."

"It does." I nod. "But not horrible, just…strange."

Maxine smiles wistfully as Gerrie plays a power chord.

"I can't have children."

"Oh." I am at a loss for what to say next. "Sorry."

She waves away my apology.

"No problem. Ace is perfect for me. He doesn't want kids because he spent too many years helping to raise his brothers and sisters. We're happy enough, it's just that I would have liked to have had the choice about whether I bring children into this world or not."

The band turn up the volume, causing me to raise my voice.

"Can the doctors do anything for you?"

"Not really." She shakes her head. "I was born without a womb you see, a freak of nature."

Here is a vulnerable side to Maxine that I've not seen before. I can tell that enforced childlessness has obviously affected her deeply, and decide not to ask any more questions.

We sit in silence and watch the band play, as the pub slowly fills up with its usual rowdy clientele. Meanwhile I'm determined to jettison a mental image of Maxine flying away to the opposite side of the world, firmly clutching my little Junior in her arms.

"Whereabouts is the caravan park?" I try to *not* sound as if I need to know.

Maxine sighs and looks at me with contempt.

"Right next door to the Sunday market. The caravan is opposite the site shop and has the name 'Seaview'. Don't worry Sophie, I'm not going to snatch your child away from you."

I blush, giving my thoughts away.

"I…I didn't mean …"

"Forget it." Maxine waves a hand in the air. "I've come across it too many times before. I'm doing this for the money. I will look after the baby to the best of my ability, and then give him back."

I feel mightily relieved.

"We'll have to talk about how we hand him over." I shout over the noise of the band. "We don't want the police stalking you."

"Too fucking right." Maxine nods in agreement. "What do you suggest?"

I haven't given this too much thought.

"I'll talk it over with Gerrie. We'll come up with something. You'll maybe have to leave him somewhere and drive off. Meanwhile I'll be watching and pick him up after you've gone. We'll have to say to the police that we don't want them following us." Maxine shouts close to my ear.

"Come up with something good. I don't want to spend the rest of my days in jail."

Chapter Twelve

I give up my supermarket job a month before the birth. It's too uncomfortable to be on my feet all day, and being on the tills is giving my wrists and hands a kind of repetitive strain injury. I sit at home as big as a barrage balloon, hating the damage to my figure, and consuming copious amounts of Easter eggs that I shouldn't really be doing. I've gained three and a half stones, and don't even want Gerrie to see me naked anymore.

Ash and Charlie pop in to see me every day, sometimes bringing things for the baby or tasty treats to eat. I'm fat, depressed about the forthcoming birth and the 'kidnapping', and my joints ache like an old woman's. Gerrie is either teaching, at Uni, or out gigging with the band. All I ever do is cook, clean, walk to the local hospital for my check-ups, or waddle to the shops. I never thought I would feel so bloody useless. I yearn for labour to commence to get Junior out of my body. Our flat is full of baby goods; a pram fills the communal hallway, but Ash and Charlie don't seem to mind. There's a cot next to my side of the bed, because we only have one bedroom.

The Braxton-Hicks contractions usually come on at night. The midwife tells me it's my body preparing for the birth, but each time I think it's the real thing and wake Gerrie up. He's getting as short-tempered as I am with the lack of sleep. I should be at Uni enjoying myself, listening to lectures, creeping along the corridors of Halls at night and sleeping around like other girls my age. I've grown up too soon. I want my mum here, but there's nowhere for her to stay and I know money is too tight for her to pay out for a hotel.

I don't think Gerrie is looking forward to the actual birth. In fact, when I think of all the pain I'll have to go through I'm right up there with him. All my old Uni friends have disappeared, and my world has shrunk before my eyes. At the moment it's down to Gerrie, Ash, Charlie, Maxine, Ace, Olly, Dave and Stu – there's nobody I could ask who might want to be a willing birth partner. Gerrie has the job of holding my hand during the birth, but I know he doesn't really want to.

"*Gerrie,* Gerrie, wake up." I prod the sleeping log next to me. "The bed's all wet! My waters have broken!"

Gerrie leaps out from under the covers like a thing possessed. It's twelve minutes past midnight on April 10th 1998, and at last little Junior is getting impatient to be free.

"I'll phone for a taxi!" He stumbles into his clothes, rubbing sleep from his eyes.

"Let me get dressed first." I heave my unwieldy body out of bed. "The baby won't be here just yet."

I am surprisingly calm, considering that I am in labour. Light contractions wash over me, and I notice a small amount of blood down the toilet pan. After padding myself up and putting on a tent-like dress and boots, I pack some last minute things into my case and take some small sips of water.

"Okay, I'm ready."

The taxi doesn't take long to arrive, and I time some mild contractions coming about every six or seven minutes. I walk with difficulty to the taxi in-between pains, and feel strangely excited. Gerrie isn't really saying much at all, but holds my hand and grabs my case as the taxi speeds off and pulls up outside the maternity entrance to our hospital in record time. There's a wheelchair in the foyer, and I'm glad to flop down into it. Gerrie wheels me to Reception, and I pray they don't send me home again. Luckily we're taken straight upstairs to the Delivery Suite, where a midwife greets me, still smiling although it's now one o'clock in the morning.

"Mrs Hermann. I'll show you to your room. I'm Julie – I'll be here until our shift changes at half past seven."

I'm surprised at how homely the room feels, even though there's a hospital bed in place and all the usual accompanying medical paraphernalia. Gerrie has to wait outside while I put on a gown to be examined. Thankfully Julie waits until there's a gap between contractions to stick a gloved finger where a gloved finger doesn't usually go.

"You're three centimetres dilated. A while to go yet, but you're doing very well. I'm going to put a monitor on you so that we can make sure baby is not getting distressed." She points downwards. "There's a call button down by the side of the bed just in case you want me. Please don't eat or drink anything, but instead I'll get the doctor to put a cannula in the back of your hand and hook you up to a glucose drip to avoid dehydration."

Gerrie comes back in, but looks terribly out of place. I know he wants to be anywhere but here, preferably on a stage somewhere, but I do my best to give him a broad smile. I hope he doesn't faint and slide down the wall.

"I'm okay. We've just got to wait it out."

He looks miserable.

"For how long?"

"As long as it takes."

He nods and sits in an armchair next to my bed. I watch time pass on the huge clock hanging on the wall opposite. The contractions carry on, some of them a little more intense. I try to stem a wave of panic in case the pain is too severe to cope with. When the doctor comes in to insert the cannula I can only manage a grimace while suffering through a particularly nasty contraction.

"Do you have anything for the pain please?"

I want to cry – I've never felt anything like this before. My abdomen is rigid. It's horrible. I want to go home.

"You can have gas and air, or I'll write you up for some pethidine, but you'll have to stay on the bed once you've had it. Your notes say that you do not want any kind of numbing epidural?"

"That's right, just pethidine, and just so long as it's *soon*."

Julie arrives with her needle and syringe. I notice Gerrie looks away as she injects something wonderful into my buttocks. The pain recedes, but I cannot open my eyes properly. I decide to close them and be done with it.

I wake up as a powerful contraction hits me. I scream with the pain, and Gerrie stops snoring and leaps out of his chair.

"I'll call the midwife!"

I'm aware he's running out of the door and shouting down the corridor. I'm frightened; my body is doing horrible things out of my control. Four hours have passed since I last looked at the clock, and Junior is impatient.

"Don't go!" I yell. "Please don't leave me!"

Two midwives come into the room, with Gerrie walking slowly behind them. I know I've got to have another examination, but Julie is as gentle as she can be under the circumstances.

"Eight centimetres – nearly time to push but not quite. We can't give you any more pethidine, but you can have gas and air if you want."

I nod through my tears and am given a rubber mask attached to a tube.

Julie takes hold of my hand.

"Breathe away any time you want to. I'm going to hand you over to Linda because my shift is over. Baby will be here quite soon, so don't worry. You're doing wonderfully well. Linda will stay here with you now."

I grab Gerrie's hand when another wave of pain washes over me, and he puts the mask over my nose and mouth.

"Breathe in Soph, come on."

I take some deep breaths and retch.

"I can't!" I fling the mask away. "It's' making me sick!"

There is nothing for it but to endure. I cry and scream and cling onto Gerrie for comfort. His tee-shirt is soaked with my tears and his sweat, but he is a comforting presence. Linda places a cold flannel over my forehead, which is balm. My body is on fire. I fling off the gown, haul myself up on my knees, and care not one jot that I am butt naked.

"I need to poo really badly!"

Linda's finger is not as gentle as Julie's, but she says those magic words that mean there is a light at the end of the tunnel.

"Lie back down Mrs Hermann and bring your knees up to your chest. When the next contraction comes, then you can push that baby out!"

And push him out I do within the following thirty minutes. My little Brett Junior slides out without a fuss at 07:52, all seven pounds two ounces of him, and with a shock of dark hair just like his father's. He is placed, wet and squealing on my collapsed abdomen, which I am dismayed to see now resembles a half-filled sack of potatoes. I stroke my baby's head and am ecstatic – there's no other word for it. Then it's time for Linda to expertly cut the cord and wrap Junior in a towel. Gerrie holds our son while my feet are placed in horrible stirrups so I can be stitched up by the doctor. Gerrie kisses me, and then I watch him and Junior gazing at each other in admiration.

I am a mother.

Chapter Thirteen

For somebody who wasn't keen on having children, Gerrie

is doing a grand job as a father. There's no Uni as it's the Easter holidays, and so it's just me, Gerrie and Junior together in our little flat, all cosy and snug. Ash and Charlie have been up to have a peep at the baby, but mostly they've left us alone. Gerrie has taken hundreds of photos of Junior with the camera, and when he goes back to Uni next week I know he'll be showing them off to anybody and everybody.

We're both totally besotted with our son. Gerrie even takes his turn with the night feeds. However, always at the back of my mind is the reality that I'll have to hand my baby over to Maxine on the 24th April, a woman who cannot have children. The prospect frightens me beyond belief, and only misery will come of it I'm sure.

My parents make the trip in their Ford Mondeo to cuddle their first grandchild. Mum cries, and Dad pats Gerrie on the back. I remind Dad that I am the one who has endured childbirth, but it's nice to be with Mum even for a short while when Dad and Gerrie go out to 'wet the baby's head'. They leave for home the next morning, and I find bags of baby clothes and formula milk have appeared that were certainly not there before. I suppose they will come in handy for Maxine and Ace.

Junior is a good little eater – slurping bottles of milk down to the last drop and sleeping the regulation four hours in between feeds. He doesn't even wake up when Gerrie is teaching – I think he must be used to loud guitar riffs because of all the gigs I attended while pregnant. I want to hold his little warm body close to me forever and never let him go.

When the baby is nearly two weeks old we make a call to Gaborone. Junior sits on my lap, dressed in a little blue Babygro and a white cardigan that I managed to knit without dropping a stitch. He sleeps soundly and looks utterly adorable.

Eila picks up the phone.

"Hi!" Gerrie sounds excited. "Guess what?"

"What?" Eila chuckles.

"You're a grandmother again." Gerrie kisses the top of Junior's head. "One day you'll meet little Brett Stephen Hermann."

There is a brief silence while Eila digests her son's news. Then she speaks.

"I have a grandson?"

"You sure do!" I shout. "Brett, or Junior as he's known."

EI can hear Eila launching into Afrikaans. Brett does a running translation, a little nervously I think.

"She's saying to Dad that he needs to stop being a miserable old bugger and to come speak to us."

And to my surprise Brett senior wants to speak to *me*. I'm a bit lost for words as I take the receiver..

"He's got Gerrie's blue eyes and brown hair."

My words seem to do the trick. Brett's stern voice softens somewhat.

"Congratulations. I'm sure he's a sturdy boy."

I'm glad he has decided to speak English –perhaps I'm not invisible after all. I nod and hand the phone back to Gerrie, and

Junior makes some little baby noises in the background, which I hope will go down well with Gerrie's' parents. Gerrie smiles at me as he carries on the conversation with his father.

"He's feeding very well and putting on weight. Dad, we named him after you."

There's silence before I hear Brett's strident tones.

"So I hear. Congratulations again to the two of you."

He goes, and we spend a few more moments talking to Eila before we end the call. Gerrie gives a low whistle.

"Whew! That didn't go too badly, did it?"

I give Gerrie a kiss, pleased for him.

"He'll come around eventually, I'm sure."

"But not soon enough." Gerrie replies wryly. "We've got to go through with the kidnap, Soph. The band is depending on me to get that money. It's our chance to be famous; we'll never get this opportunity again."

My heart sinks as Junior's tiny finger curls around my own. I don't think I can do it.

I open the front door to Maxine and Ace, who call round on the evening of 23rd April.

"Hi." I greet them. "Come up. Gerrie's got the kettle on."

I follow them upstairs with a heavy heart. Gerrie brings a tray of coffee into the front room and we sit in silence, each waiting for the other to speak. Ace ventures a few words.

"So…what's happening tomorrow?"

"No more telephone calls for a start." Gerrie takes a biscuit. "I've found out that Charlie and Ash who live downstairs are both on nights for this coming week. Whatever we do has got to be at night when they're not here."

"Okay." Ace nods. "I'll come and pick Junior up and any baby stuff you want me to take about midnight tomorrow?"

I want to scream. *This cannot be happening!* Maxine looks at Junior, safe in my arms.

"Can I hold him?"

I keep a firm grip on my baby, but Gerrie manages to diffuse the situation.

"You can tomorrow. Right now Sophie's a bit upset about the whole thing."

Maxine nods in sympathy.

"Oh. Sorry Soph."

I wipe away a tear, but can find no voice. However, Gerrie has enough words for both of us.

"Go straight to the caravan and stay there for the whole week. I'll phone Dad the next day and of course the police. I'll write a ransom note. Next Saturday night at seven o'clock bring him to the pub where we sometimes practise – you know Ace, The Standard. Maxine can leave him in his car seat inside the ladies' toilets. One of us will be there to pick him up."

I clutch Junior ever tighter to my chest, who begins to wail. I stand up and make my way to the fridge to get one of his bottles of milk. Nobody follows me, and I have a last minute bonding session with my baby. I only hope he remembers who his mother is.

Gerrie almost has to wrestle the baby out of my arms the following night. Ace loads up his car and then stands in the front room with Maxine waiting for me to loosen my grip on Junior in the bedroom next door, who with a stomach full of milk, sleeps the slumber of the innocent.

"It's just for a week. Dad'll pay up. Come on Soph, they're waiting."

He puts his arm around the two of us and I burst into floods of tears as I reluctantly hand over my precious warm bundle.

"I'm staying here in bed." I sob. "I can't bear to see him go."

"Neither can I." Gerrie takes Junior from me and kisses the top of his head. "But there's no other way. I'm going to take a photo of him before they go."

There's a muted conversation out in the hallway, then the sound of footsteps on the stairs. A car starts up directly outside and joins other midnight traffic on the Blackhorse Road. Gerrie comes back into the bedroom, undresses, and gets into bed beside me. Tears are on his cheeks. We fall sobbing into each other's arms. We are bereft. His cot is empty. It actually feels as though our baby *has* been kidnapped.

Chapter Fourteen

"*Where* was the baby when you last saw him yesterday?"

I cannot stop crying. We've made a terrible mistake. I face the constable and policewoman and try to speak the rehearsed lines through genuine tears.

"He fell asleep in his pushchair. We'd been out walking to try and get him to sleep. Gerrie carried the pram upstairs and put it in the front room. We thought we'd leave Junior in there rather than risk waking him up and putting him in his cot. When I woke up about three o'clock and got out of bed to check on him, he was gone."

The policewoman nods and jots down some notes.

"Had the front door been forced?"

I don't know if the officers believe us or not. I hope for the best and carry on blindly.

"*Our* door was open, but the main door to the street was closed."

The constable looks around our untidy front room and then speaks to Gerrie.

"Why would anybody want to break in and take your baby?"

Gerrie sighs. He looks as terrible as I feel.

"My parents are rich. I expect somebody knows this and might be demanding lots of money in the near future."

There is a glimmer of comprehension as the two officers exchange a quick glance. The policewoman scribbles furiously before looking up at us.

"Have you heard from the kidnappers?"

"No." Gerrie shakes his head. "Not yet."

The constable makes his way out onto the landing before turning back towards us.

"We'll get a forensics team round here, and also get a tap on your phone. Officer Judith Farrow will stay here for now in case there's a ransom demand. Meanwhile we'll speak to your neighbours downstairs, and get a team out to search the local area with the dogs. Please can I have a photo and something your baby has been wearing recently?"

I bring a couple of Gerrie's many photographs, together with a soiled Babygro, and a milk spattered matinee jacket from the laundry basket. They smell of Junior, which makes the tears flow freely again.

"He wore these last." I sob as I hand over the clothing and cuddle up to Gerrie. "Please bring us back our baby."

It's difficult trying to talk to Gerrie with Judith listening to every word we say. We didn't envisage a policewoman actually living with us. Gerrie announces he's going out to do his own search, but I know he wants some privacy to talk on his mobile to his father. I have to stay indoors by the landline phone. The flat is suddenly full of men in white boiler suits taking fingerprints. I daren't make any more calls on the landline. Nowhere is private.

At the end of that first day Judith makes herself comfortable on our settee, and Gerrie and I have a chance to whisper to each other as we lie in bed. I shuffle over to his pillow and get as close to Gerrie's ear as I can.

"What did you say to your dad?"

"I told him the baby has been abducted and that we're waiting to hear more."

"And?"

Gerrie looks fixedly up at the ceiling before whispering a reply.

"*And*…I discovered he doesn't believe in paying out ransom money."

"What!" I hiss. "He won't pay to get his grandson back?"

"Nope." Gerrie sighs. "He said that if he pays out for Junior, then he'll probably get another three kidnapped granddaughters as well."

"So what's the point of going on with this?" I whisper in the darkness. "Let's just wait until Ace and Maxine bring Junior back on Saturday."

Gerrie puts an arm around my shoulders and pulls me towards him.

"No, let's carry on as planned. Dad might change his mind. Early in the morning I'll go down to get the milk and then bring back the note I've left under the carpet by the front door. We can call Mum and Dad then, with Judith listening in."

Neither of us can sleep. We huddle together and wait for the dawn. I try not to think of Maxine holding Junior in her arms – it's just too painful.

Soon after 6am Gerrie creeps downstairs. As he comes back up I can hear Judith moving about in the room next door. I put on a dressing gown and Judith follows me out to the kitchen. Gerrie joins us, holding two pints of milk and a piece of paper.

"This was with the milk."

Judith scans the paper.

"They want forty five thousand pounds and no newspaper coverage or police involvement."

"Speak to your dad on your phone, Gerrie." I'm shaking with nerves because this whole scenario is not turning out as it should. "Do you think he'll pay the money?"

Gerrie opens one of the milk bottles and tries to pretend he doesn't already know the answer.

"I'll call him, just as soon as I've had a coffee. Judith, you can see they don't want the police here. I'd rather you managed operations from your station if you don't mind."

"I'll check with my team." Judith nods. "Sophie, try and stay calm if you can."

I wipe away some tears.

"I'll try, but have you ever had your baby taken away? If so, you'll know why I'm shaking."

Judith pats my arm.

"I'll have a quick shower, then I'll make a few phone calls and see what's happening."

As soon as Judith drives away, we call Gaborone and Eila answers at once. She sounds desperate, as though she has been awake all night.

"Hello. Any news from the kidnappers?" She sounds genuinely concerned.

"Yes." I reply quickly. "They want forty five thousand pounds and no police or Press involvement."

Brett takes over the conversation and wants to speak directly to Gerrie. It's a good thing my father-in-law has a loud voice. After I've passed the phone over I can still hear every word he says.

"Son, I've already explained why I cannot pay the ransom."

Beside me I can see Gerrie's hands balling into fists.

"Dad, we're desperate. There's nobody else we can ask. We won't see Junior again unless they get their money."

Brett says something to Gerrie in Afrikaans, and then there is silence. Gerrie ends the call, and I turn to him.

"What did your father say?"

He shrugs.

"He asked if the tour fees had increased. I don't think he believes us, Soph."

My husband has a defeated air about him. Brett has scuppered our plans, and there is nothing for it but to wait until Saturday evening to get Junior back. I ache to speak to Maxine, but know that our landline is tapped, and that the police will probably be tracing any call I make on my mobile.

Meanwhile we have to make an effort to search for our son. Judith lets us know that the dog teams have so far been unsuccessful. I reluctantly inform her that Junior's grandfather refuses to pay a penny in ransom and that therefore we are utterly stymied. Once again there is mention of getting TV and newspapers involved. I tell Judith to wait until the following Monday and then to go ahead.

And so transpires the longest week I have ever spent. Search teams engaged on their unwittingly fruitless task report back regularly with no sightings. I walk around in a daze of despair, my arms physically aching to hold my baby. Gerrie goes back to Uni after the Easter break and tries in vain to study for his finals. *Death Throes* remind us of the deadline for paying the tour money.   Ace is holed up in Felixstowe, and so the band cannot practise without their lead singer. To top it all, there are no phone calls to or from Gaborone.

To have spent nine months incubating a little person, giving birth and bonding with him, and then to have him taken away such a short time afterwards brings deep, dark feelings of grief that I had never previously experienced. I cannot sleep for those first few nights, and spend hours staring at the ceiling. Gerrie has to physically stop me packing a bag and leaving for Felixstowe.

After a few days Judith leaves the flat and Gerrie and I heave a sigh of relief. We have our privacy again, but still do not dare to phone Ace or Maxine. We keep up the appearance of grieving parents, which is absolutely genuine grief on my part. As time moves agonisingly slowly towards Saturday evening the black cloud of doom hanging over our heads begins to lift, and I cannot wait to see Junior's little face again.

Chapter Fifteen

$\mathcal{W}e$ sit in a corner booth at The Standard, quite near the ladies' lavatory on Saturday evening at the appointed time, in fact a little early. I am excited to see if Junior has grown in the time he has been away. There is another band sound-checking on stage, and their classic covers are more to my liking. I hum along to Wishbone Ash's 'Blowin' Free'. Gerrie gives my shoulder a squeeze.

"You've cheered up today."

"Why d'you think that is?" I chuckle. "My little Junior is coming back to his mummy."

"And his daddy." Gerrie reminds me. "I love him too."

We sip our drinks and keep an eye on the door. At five minutes to seven a blast of cool air rushes in as a couple enter and I immediately stand up, but to my disappointment it's not Ace or Maxine. Dismayed, I sink down and look at my phone as seven o'clock goes past and then five past seven. Gerrie tries to calm my nerves.

"They might have got held up in traffic."

I stand up again and go into the toilet just to see if Maxine has already been and gone, but the cubicles are empty. A sinking feeling clutches at my heart and will not let go. When I emerge into the bar, Gerrie is still sitting there on his own. I flop down next to him anxiously, impatient for the sight of my baby.

"Can we phone them?

"Only if there's a payphone here." Gerrie looks around. "The police can trace any call we make on our mobiles."

I can see a payphone on the wall by the toilets. I search through my phone to find Maxine's number.

"Have you got some change?" I ask Gerrie. "I've only got a note."

Armed with a handful of coins, I dial Maxine's mobile number. There is a disconnected tone. I try Ace, but the same thing happens. Worried, I go back to Gerrie.

"Their phones aren't working." My voice rises in panic. "They're not coming!"

Gerrie pulls me down next to him.

"It's only quarter past. Let's give them until eight o'clock. They're bound to be here by then."

We sit there until closing time, growing increasingly desperate. I feel powerless. I want my baby so much it's like a physical pain in the guts. By eleven o'clock Gerrie has sunk too many beers, and is morose. We walk home disconsolately along the Blackhorse Road, and Gerrie stumbles a little bit.

"I'm going to ring the police first thing in the morning. We'll go to the TV, radio, newspapers, and anybody else who wants to know." I take his arm and hold him up. "Junior really *has* been kidnapped now. I *knew* we shouldn't have handed over the baby to Maxine. She can't have children – it's obvious she wouldn't be able to resist taking him once she'd looked after him for a few hours."

"It's all my fault." Gerrie mumbles. "I'm such a fucking arsehole. I told you I was at the beginning before we'd even got married."

"I love you anyway." I kiss his cheek. "Just don't puke all over me."

I unlock our front door and help Gerrie up the stairs. He flops onto the bed fully clothed and falls asleep immediately. I lie wide awake beside him, mentally trying to tune into my baby's thought waves (if indeed he has any), while tears stream down my cheeks.

I've always wondered what it would be like to appear on TV, but I never thought it would be like this. Press cameras flash before my eyes as I blink in their light and haltingly read the autocue. A recent photo of Junior is shown in the background and Gerrie's arm is comforting around my shoulders, but it doesn't take away the frustrating fact that we cannot name Ace and Maxine and have it known that we have engineered our own baby's disappearance. It is also patently clear that it's not worth mentioning their names anyway, as neither of us know Ace's real Christian name or either of their surnames.

"If anyone has seen our baby or know who has kidnapped him, please ring the number at the bottom of the screen." I wipe my eyes before continuing. "Junior is very precious to us. We want him back."

I fervently hope that Maxine is watching somewhere and can see my genuine distress. I quiz Gerrie on our return to the flat.

"What's Ace's surname?"

Gerrie shrugs.

"Who knows? Blokes don't bother talking about things like that."

$\mathcal{The}$ police search steps up a gear. After appearing on another TV news bulletin, we become infamous as the couple whose baby is missing. Mum and Dad drive up with their Ford Mondeo the following Friday night and put themselves at our disposal for the whole weekend. We inform Brett and Eila when our TV appeals are due to be scheduled and they realise that the situation is serious, but still no ransom money appears. Members of the public call and keep the police busy following up fruitless leads.

We are still of the opinion that we cannot incriminate ourselves and tell the truth. However, there are two people that I *can* trust in this world – the people who have made the 200 mile journey to help us. We tell the whole story to Mum and Dad, who sit in our front room and listen attentively. Mum takes hold of my hand and is her usual non-judgemental self.

"What we'll do tomorrow is make the journey to Felixstowe and find that caravan."

I nod. I'd been thinking along the same lines.

"Maxine had told me it's the site next to the Sunday market, near the beach. We'll ask at Reception to see if they'll let us look inside the caravan – it's called *Seaview*."

"Might be best just to ask any neighbours whether they've seen anybody in there." Gerrie appears thoughtful. "The staff might alert the police."

Dad chips in with an idea of his own.

"We might even be able to look in one of the windows if nobody's about."

We set off early on the Saturday morning for the 90 mile journey to the East coast. We locate the site without too much trouble, and there's a chilly wind whipping around our legs as we get out of the car well away from Reception.

"Maxine said the caravan is opposite the shop." I pull my coat around me. "Let's walk a bit."

We blend in with other early holidaymakers, and nobody really gives us a second glance. The season is just getting underway, and many of the caravans are in need of a spruce-up, including *Seaview* when we eventually find it. Green algae sprouts on the outside decking, and the caravan has an unused air to it. Gerrie is first up the steps and peering in through the windows.

"Nobody's been here for months." He turns towards me as I join him on the decking. "There's a big plate of what looks like salt on the table."

"That's to absorb any moisture." Dad walks along to look in another window. "We used to put plates of salt out during the winter when my parents had their caravan years ago."

"Would anybody else know Ace's surname?" I ask Gerrie. "The other band members? Is Ace his real name?"

"Nobody in the band would know." Gerrie shrugs. "I told you – blokes don't care about names. We only know him as Ace."

I leave them to it and walk across to the shop, where a rather bored-looking young woman is serving behind the counter.

"Hi." I smile at her. "Have you seen a chap with long hair and a red-headed woman with a baby recently using the caravan opposite?"

"'Fraid not." The girl shakes her head. "We've not long opened after the winter break. There's hardly anyone here at the moment."

Another theory falls through. We've wasted a whole morning that we'll never get back again, and still our baby remains missing.

It's not until we're back in the car that I have a brainwave.

"Shall we ask Reception who owns Seaview?"

Mum and Dad look at each other, and then at Gerrie, who nods.

"It sounds like a good idea. Let's pretend we want to buy it."

We decide that Mum and Dad should go in and ask, as they look more likely to have the money behind them to buy a caravan. Gerrie and I sit in the car and stare at the salesman behind the counter, trying to read his lips. When my parents return I look at them inquisitively.

"Well?"

"Nobody owns it." Mum gives me an apologetic look. "It's old and due to be taken off site. When I asked for the previous owners' names, the chap clammed up due to data protection."

"How can we tell this to Judith?" I sigh. "She'll wonder why we're interested in a caravan in Felixstowe."

Gerrie shakes his head.

"Don't bother. If it's Maxine's parents they'll just protect her and we'll be no further forward. She probably hasn't told them where she is anyway."

I want to cry with frustration because I know he's right. Another idea has come to nought.

Three weeks later _Death Throes_ inform Gerrie that they've found another support band. Stu and Dave begin to phone us constantly as to Ace's whereabouts and the upcoming tour dates. Gerrie lets them down gently, but he's not really bothered anymore about band practise. He takes his mock exams during May and the first part of June whilst still teaching his pupils, and just about manages to scrape by. His thoughts are elsewhere, just as mine are. I return to the supermarket to try and take my mind off the fact that our baby is growing up day by day and little by little without his parents who love him.

Towards the end of June the phone rings one evening while we are watching ourselves on TV taking part in yet another news bulletin. I pick up the receiver.

"Hello?"

"It's Eila. How are things with you?"

I sigh.

"No news I'm afraid. The police usually let us know of any leads, but I don't think there's as many as there used to be."

"I'm so sorry." Eila's voice appears to crack. "Can Brett have a word with Gerrie please?"

There's a conversation in rapid Afrikaans. At the end of it I'm surprised to see Gerrie put down the receiver and then sob, with his head in his hands. I run to him.

"What's wrong?"

It's some time before he speaks, but when he does his words bring tears to my own eyes.

"Dad's transferred forty-five thousand pounds to my bank account today. He said we'd be welcome any time back home at Gaborone".

We have our tour money, but with nobody to pay it to. We've missed the boat. I contact Judith and let her know we will give the money to anybody who can find our son. A news bulletin with this information sends another flurry of leads that keep the police busy and give us false hope. However, each lead brings us crashing down. It appears to all intents and purposes, that Ace and Maxine have disappeared off the face of the earth.

The reality of what might have happened hits us after we have watched our teary selves yet again on TV. The story following ours centres on information concerning passports, and that photos and details of children will need to be added to parents' passports from October. When Junior went missing it was only April. I look at Gerrie in alarm.

"Do you think they've spirited him thousands of miles away to another country, maybe even using false passports?"

I dread hearing his reply, but I listen all the same.

"Probably." Gerrie sighs. "Ace knows a lot of shady characters. They all hang around his block of flats at night. How d'you think he got an MOT certificate for that old banger of his?"

That's it; we're stuffed. We can't tell the police, and if Ace and Maxine are using false names anyway, what's the point? I'm coming to the conclusion we'll never find them now.

Chapter Sixteen

$\mathcal{As}$ the weeks go by with no sightings of our son, Gerrie loses

all hope and begins to sink into a well of depression. I try and encourage him to study for his final exams to take his mind off the fact that he's blaming himself for the mess we're in and for letting the band down, despite me peering into every pram I pass to see if my baby is in there. He does make a half-hearted attempt, with the result that his efforts are just enough to scrape by again with the lowest level of pass.

However, he doesn't care that he now has his music degree and that he could apply for a teaching post. He shaves his head and puts away his guitar. Dave and Stu stop contacting him. Summer moves into autumn. He cannot sleep at night, and his weight drops from a sturdy 14 stone to just over 11. He is a shadow of his former self. I hardly recognise him.

Adversity has a strange effect on people. I find an inner strength I didn't know I had, and although I'm dying inside with longing to see my baby I have to prop Gerrie up and somehow keep him going. I realise he needs medical help, but he refuses to see a doctor.

Nobody comes forward with any knowledge of Junior's whereabouts. We have no idea where to look and have to rely on the police following up leads. I'm looking as hard as I can every time I go out the door, but am mindful that I mustn't sink into Gerrie's well of hopelessness. Life has to go on and we have to eat. We decide to dip into the ransom money just a little bit in order to live a frugal lifestyle, augmented by my wages from the supermarket. Some days Gerrie just lies on the settee all day, motionless and distraught. He forbids me to contact his parents, and their calls to him go unanswered.

I lie awake next to him at night as he tosses and turns, and wrack my brain to think of something to bring him out of his misery. The only thing I can think of is that which he loves the best; music. I search the jobs market and find an advert for a junior lecturer/sound engineer at the very university he has not long left. I show him the advert, but it fails to elicit the interest I'd hoped for. I send off his CV and hope for the best.

One day after work I walk along the High Street to the music shop which used to be Gerrie's second home, and stand there looking at adverts for band members pinned on a worn-out cork board. There's a Georgie looking for a rock guitarist. I stand in the street and phone the number.

"Yeah?"

The voice is deep and with a distinct South London accent.

"Have you found a guitarist?"

"Nah." Georgie replies. "We want a guy to play lead. I can only do rhythm."

I stick my neck out and hope Gerrie won't kill me.

"Come round and see my husband in about an hour. He once had a chance to tour with *Death Throes*."

"Yeah?"

I have won Georgie's interest. I give him our address and tell him to bring his guitar. I fish Gerrie's guitar out of the back of his wardrobe and wake him up from his stupor.

"There's a guy coming to see you. He wants you to play lead guitar in his band."

"Well, he can piss right off." Gerrie looks at his guitar in my hands. "Why have you got that out?"

"He'll be here soon to do a bit of jamming with you, so you'd better remember some rock solos."

I thrust the guitar at him. To my surprise he takes it and puts it on his lap. I go into the kitchen to prepare dinner and leave him to it. After about ten minutes I can hear strains of the solo from the Eagles' *'Hotel California'* filtering out of the front room.

Georgie is a breath of fresh air. Within half an hour he has Gerrie making his dusty Gibson Flying V cry and sing. There is the wisp of a smile on his face as he does it. I thank the Lord for the Georgies of this world. *Princes of Darkness* is just a pub band, but then again so was *Thrash* at the start. Gerrie gets the job.

To my surprise and his, he also gets an interview for the junior lecturer post. He berates me for sending off his CV without his knowledge, but inside I think he is secretly pleased. The staff there already know him from his studies, and so realise what he is capable of and that he is already a highly respected sound engineer.

Thin, shaven-headed and pale, Gerrie attends for an interview in his best suit, which hangs off him. Whether they give him the job because they have seen the news bulletins and can see he is suffering over the loss of his son, I don't know. All that I *do* know is that I am eternally grateful he secures the post. The job and the new band give him the uplift he so desperately needs. He starts to eat regular meals and he sleeps more soundly at night. We still cry together sometimes when we realise we are missing Junior's first steps and his first words, but harsh reality brings us to the conclusion that sooner or later life has to carry on. We decide the best thing to do is to try for another baby, which strangely enough doesn't seem to be as easy to put into motion as the first time. However, I am ever hopeful.

A year on from the kidnapping and I have a desperate need to work with children, especially toddlers of the same age that Junior now is. When it is obvious to us that our son is not coming back, I take the necessary business studies and childcare exam courses and buy a suitable industrial unit nearby with what is left of the tour/ransom money. The interest it has gathered is enough to make the first monthly repayment on a business loan. I transform the unit into a nursery and employ two wonderful members of staff, Mollie and Deirdre. We welcome our first infant customer and word soon spreads. Being busy helps me to forget the pain of losing Junior. My arms need to be filled with children; it is the best remedy for me. We open during school term times only, and before long I have three members of staff and twelve little darlings to look after.

Chapter Seventeen

The Embankment is packed; people stand ten deep waiting for the magic hour. Street parties and funfairs are going on all around us. As much as I could never envision the twentieth century ever ending, the actual moment is almost with us when Big Ben will strike out the old year and bring in the new.

My legs ache. We've been standing watching the lights of the Festival Hall on the other side of the river and the newly installed Millennium Wheel for nearly four hours since the police closed off all the side roads leading down to the river. Being in the front row we've also got a good view of all the riverboats, which are now jostling for position to be as near to the *'River of Fire'* firework display as they can possibly get. Some people are climbing up onto the boats' rooves. I hope and pray they are not too inebriated and end up in the river.

The river police patrol up and down on the water looking for trouble, and I'm slightly irritated that a security guard is standing facing the crowd almost opposite where we're standing. He's a big chap and he's blocking some of the view. The crowd are good-natured and are waiting patiently, so I don't really see the need for him to stare at us so intensely.

The atmosphere is electric as the crowd begin to count down the last minute in time with the seconds being projected onto the front façade of the Oxo Tower across the river. Big Ben's sonorous tones suddenly cause my eyes to fill with tears and make me feel proud that London is my hometown.

As the first dong of midnight sounds, the crowd erupt, a cacophony of foghorns sound on the river, and the much anticipated *River of Fire* explodes in a colourful pyrotechnic delight. Five minutes into the display and ignoring the security guard, Gerrie pulls me towards him and kisses me soundly on the lips.

"Happy New Year, Soph. I love you."

My tears fall freely at his words. I wait for a particularly loud rocket to end its skyward path, and move closer to Gerrie's ear.

"I love you too. I have some good news already for the New Year."

He looks at me quizzically.

"Yeah?"

"Yes." I nod. "I'm pregnant!"

Gerrie envelops me in a bear hug and lifts me off the floor, shouting to the world over an accompanying burst of thunderous firecrackers.

"My wife's pregnant!"

"Put me down!" I shout at him, embarrassed.

"Yeah!" A male voice shouts from behind. "Well done mate!"

I am lowered to the ground as though I am made of glass. Grinning, we stand with our arms around each other to enjoy the rest of the fireworks. Somehow I know that the year 2000 will be a turning point for us.

At twenty past midnight there is a rush of people waving football rattles and shouting pleasantries to all and sundry trying to exit the Embankment and make their way up to the Strand to hopefully catch the last train from Charing Cross. Gerrie and I find a non-barricaded road and wait patiently in the queue. Gerrie kisses the top of my head and laughs.

"You kept that quiet."

"I wanted to surprise you." I smile at him. "The doctor confirmed it yesterday. Our little bundle of joy is going to have Mummy watching its every move. Ace and Maxine will not be taking *this* one away from us."

The queue shuffles forward and we slip past the police barricades. Gerrie gives me a squeeze.

"We must be careful not to mollycoddle him or her too much, Soph."

I know he's right, but the urge to press my new-born baby to my chest and never let it go is very strong. We stroll through the crowds back to our room at the Strand Palace Hotel, happier than we have been for ages. I give a little shiver of anticipation knowing that nobody, *absolutely nobody*, is ever going to take my second child away from me.

"**Mrs** Hermann, I can hear two heartbeats."

I'm flabbergasted as I sit up and face the midwife, who puts down her ear trumpet and beams me a big smile.

"Twins? I'm having twins?"

The midwife nods.

"We'll do your scan now to confirm it, but I'm not usually wrong."

I wonder how to tell Gerrie that we'll need to move out of our little flat.

"I thought I was getting rather big a bit too soon compared to last time."

"Oh." The midwife checks through my notes. "Yes I thought from my examination that you'd already had a baby, although you didn't say."

I bite my lip. In my haste I had forgotten that Gerrie and I had agreed not to mention Brett.

"He was kidnapped. We don't know where he is. I'd rather not talk about it."

"Sorry." The midwife nods sympathetically and rubs some gel onto my bare abdomen. "Well, now you've got two to make up for it."

How can having two babies make up for the one that is lost? Until my dying breath I will think about Junior and wonder what happened to him. *Even if I have another six children the pain will never go away.*

I look up at the monitor as the probe moves slowly over my ever-growing bump. Sure enough even I with a limited medical knowledge can pick out two heads and a tangle of little arms and legs. The midwife, happy in her diagnosis, glances away from the monitor towards me.

"Would you like to know the sex of the babies?"

"Yes please." I nod. "It'll help if one of them is a girl, as then I'll know to buy some more clothes. I already have boys' things."

The midwife gazes at the screen for a few minutes before replying.

"You have one of each. Congratulations Mrs Hermann."

I leave the hospital in a daze. I cannot wait for the babies to arrive and fill my empty arms. I have the nursery of course, but it doesn't come close to having your own children to love and care for. I make a mental note to promote Deirdre and train her up; I will need to take my full quota of maternity leave.

"*You're* joking!" Gerrie's fork stops halfway to his mouth.

"Nope. You're going to be a daddy to two babies instead of one, and probably sooner than you think. The midwife said that a twin pregnancy doesn't usually go to full term."

"Fuckadoodledo!"

We laugh together and nearly choke on our chicken salad. Gerrie reads my mind.

"We're going to have to move out of this flat. There's not enough room here for two cots, two high chairs, and a double buggy."

"Er…I was going to mention that." I sigh. "But you beat me to it. Do you want to stay round here in Walthamstow?"

Gerrie shakes his head.

"No, I think it's time to move and get a mortgage. Now my citizenship's been agreed, it should be a lot easier. What about Chingford? It's not too far away, so will be ideal for work for both of us."

"Yes that's a good option." I nod. "I've been there quite often. We're earning good money, so the repayments shouldn't be a problem. I'll miss Ash and Charlie though."

"They can come and visit." Gerrie replies. "I'm sure they'd love to babysit."

"No babysitters." I state firmly. "If we go out, the kids come too."

The agent from Price & King takes a quick look at my burgeoning stomach as he unlocks the door to an empty terraced house halfway along Bingham Road.

"This one has two good sized bedrooms. When's the baby due?"

"Late July or early August, and there's two of them."

"Oh! Well … congratulations! Have a look around. It's only just come on the market, and it's just right for a growing family."

Our footsteps echo on bare floorboards as Gerrie and I take our time walking from room to room.

"D'you like it? It's better than all the others we've looked at." Gerrie stops in the back bedroom and looks out of the window. "The garden could do with a bit of work, but the price is ideal."

"It's great." I nod. "By the time the kids need their own bedrooms we'll be able to afford a three-bedroomed house, but for now this is what I want. If and when Junior is found then we'll have to get a bunk bed in there."

I try not to lose hope, but as time goes on it's very hard to stay positive.

I make sure we're busy moving house during those dark days leading up to Junior's second birthday, and at the end of April 2000 we're pretty well settled in. Gerrie digs over the garden and lays turves, and I prepare the twins' bedroom, ignoring various aches and pains in my lower back and legs as the babies grow ever larger inside me.

When I become too big to work I decide to take an extended maternity leave, safe in the knowledge that Deirdre will manage the nursery just fine while I'm away. I figure that when I'm ready to return, what better job is there to have than running a nursery? I will be able to take the twins with me, where they will be looked after by myself or members of my trusted staff.

I sit around the house eating foods I shouldn't eat and doing my beached whale impression. I ask the midwife if my babies could be born at home, as I have a great fear of somebody sneaking into the ward and snatching them in the night. To my delight she agrees. It's reassuring that there is a hospital nearby just in case, but I am healthy, the babies are not breech, and she does not foresee any complications during labour.

At the end of June the weather heats up and I rip off the plastic sheeting I've put on the bed to protect it, as it crinkles every time we turn over in the night and it makes us sweat. Gerrie states firmly that he doesn't care if my waters break all over the mattress – he'll just buy another one.

As it happens it's early evening on July 17th when the twins announce their imminent arrival, and I call the midwife on duty when the contractions are every ten minutes. She arrives to find I am smiling instead of screaming, happy and secure in my own home, with Gerrie on hand to help our babies into the world. Within four hours Jacob, 5lb 2 oz and Grace 5lb slide out to fill my long-empty arms. I am a mother once more.

After a short paternity leave Gerrie is home for the summer holidays, and we wallow in the pleasure of looking after our babies. At first there's the seemingly never-ending cycle of sterilising and making up bottles, feeding hungry mouths and changing nappies, but Mum arrives for a few days, sleeps on our settee, and helps us get into some sort of routine. Although tired, I am happier than I have been for a very long time.

The twins grow and put on weight. Jake is the more vociferous of the two, and looks more like Junior and Gerrie. Grace is quiet, passive, and has my eyes and mouth. I love them with a passion I never thought I'd have again after the loss of Junior.

I am a proud parent as I push my double buggy along Chingford High Street, enjoying the attention from passing strangers. Two little faces peep out from under their baby blankets, trying to make sense of the world around them. I know Junior should be toddling along holding onto the pram, but looking after the twins ensures that I am too busy to dwell on the black cloud hanging over my head that came with losing him. Jake and Grace keep thoughts of my eldest son on the back burner; he is gone, but he is definitely not forgotten. I keep a watchful eye on my babies. Gerrie says I can be likened to a lioness protecting her cubs.

The police keep us informed as to whether there are any new leads, but as time goes on I am enough of a realist to know that the chances of Junior being found are growing ever more unlikely.

Part Two – January 2017

Chapter Eighteen

The ostriches and wildebeests in particular used to hold a great attraction for Grace and Jacob, but now they're approaching seventeen all they seem to do is stare down at their phones. I look out of the observation window and wonder if the trip to Gaborone's Game Reserve has been a total waste of time. Gerrie yawns and closes his eyes against the hot African sun.

"There's some kingfishers over there." I point wildly. "Can you see them?"

Jacob's thumbs are busy killing virtual gangsters on his iPhone, and Grace I think is still scrolling through the delights that the local shopping mall has to offer.

Grace looks up at me with those wide grey eyes so like mine.

"Grandpapa's given me a hundred pounds. Can I go to Fashion World tomorrow please?"

I give up. Teenagers today don't seem to have the same interests as when Gerrie and I were young.

"Sure, but we only have two more days here before we fly back home. College starts again next week don't forget."

Jacob stops thumb twiddling long enough to give his sister a withering glance.

"I don't want to walk around boring shopping malls all day." Gerrie's patience is wearing thin, I can tell.

"Then you can stay with Grandpapa and Nana on the estate."

"No, I'll go with you lot." Jacob looks back down at his phone. "I've got a hundred pounds too, but only need to visit the sports shop."

I don't really want to go anywhere. I'm happy to stay on the estate and swim in the pool. I'm sure Gerrie feels the same. The weather's too hot for us; we're not used to it.

"We'll go to the mall in the morning and then we can spend the rest of the time back at the estate. It'll be the last chance to see your cousins too. Uncle Raymond, Aunt Valerie, and Aunt Skye and all the kids will be coming over for a barbeque tomorrow evening."

"Amahle's so beautiful." Grace sighs and runs her fingers through her mid-length brown hair. "I'll never be as pretty as her."

"That sucks." Jacob retorts drily.

Grace shoots her brother a withering look as Gerrie's phone buzzes. He reads a message and stands up.

"Come on, let's go back to the estate. Harold's outside with the car."

The air-conditioned Mercedes is wonderfully cool. I slip into the back seat and enjoy the ride back. The twins are silently sending messages to friends back in the UK, and Gerrie falls asleep. When Harold pulls up at the outer gate and speaks into the security intercom, I realise I must have been asleep too, but do not quite remember dozing off.

Eila greets us as we enter the house. I'm always amazed at how her bone structure ensures that she looks years younger than a woman now in her early-seventies. She kisses me.

"Hey! Had a good day?"

"I have, but I think the twins would rather have visited a phone shop."

Brett joins Eila in the hallway as the twins greet their grandparents and then run upstairs to the guest rooms.

"Youngsters these days don't know they're born." He watches their retreating backs fondly. "My father had me working by the time I was thirteen."

"Dinner will be in about an hour." Eila informs us. "Time for a shower I expect."

"And a doze." Gerrie yawns. "I'm forty – that's middle aged now."

"Come on Grandpa." I take my husband's hand. "Let's go and make ourselves beautiful for dinner."

Our bedroom is vast, with panoramic views over the estate. The en-suite is equipped with a bath *and* a shower, and Gerrie is already divesting himself of his clothing as he walks towards the bathroom.

"Come and get in the bath with me. No time like the present."

He opens the taps and I have a sudden flashback of the first time we ever made love; he had come off stage an hour beforehand and couldn't wait to get home and de-sweat in our little flat – in the flat where Junior was conceived that very night.

Junior. Such a long time ago. I do the maths – he would be nearly 19 now, the same age as I had been when I'd met Gerrie. Junior is often in my thoughts. Gerrie hardly ever mentions him now, but a mother never forgets the baby she carried in her womb for nine months. I even kept the Babygro that the police returned to me six months' later. It still smelt of him. I just couldn't wash it, and keep it at the back of my wardrobe at home. The twins know they have an older brother who was kidnapped, but as they've never seen him they're interested but not too bothered. I've shown them the photos that Gerrie took at the time. It seems none of us can think of him other than being a baby, but in reality he's obviously a full grown man now. I do not think of him as dead, as I know Maxine would never have let anything bad happen to him. So… somewhere out there in the world is our son, mine and Gerrie's, and all I can hope is that Maxine has a change of heart one day and tells him who his real parents are. Until she does, I don't expect he will ever know.

Maxine. My anger is still there but has dissipated somewhat over time. However, I still do not know how I'd react if I ever came across her again. I'm sure Gerrie would flatten Ace if the two of them ever met up. How have they lived with their consciences all these years, knowing that they stole somebody else's baby?

I cannot help but think back to Gerrie's breakdown after the kidnap; his guilt at sacrificing Junior to get one over on his father and the knowledge that he'd let the band down, while I had to be strong for both of us and try my best to stem his melancholia. Was it Karma that I saw the advert for a sound engineer/music lecturer at the university in time and showed it to Gerrie? How he'd hugged me and assured me he would work for as long as it took to get his life back in order! Joining *Princes of Darkness* and growing his hair again was another step in the right direction to putting a smile back on his face.

He's still smiling at me now, while scooping up handfuls of bubbles. I undress and climb into the huge claw-foot bath with my husband, and we giggle like the two teenagers we once were. I soap his chest and back and squeeze the water from his greying ponytail. I love him to the moon and back.

"How about a quick one before dinner?" Gerrie gives me a leer and a pelvic thrust, making the water splash up over the top of the bath. "What d'you say, eh?"

I laugh and move on top of him.

"Why not?"

It's bloody uncomfortable having sex in a bath. My knees prefer to squidge down into our memory foam mattress instead of having an unwelcome bony contact with hard enamel. I wish Gerrie would close his eyes sometimes and let his other senses take over, as I'm sure my thirty nine year old features aren't as delightful to him as they once were. Nevertheless, it's a pleasant way to spend ten minutes or so.

Chapter Nineteen

It's our last night at Gaborone before we fly back tomorrow.

I chat to Skye, Eila and Valerie while picking at my steak and keeping half an eye on Gerrie, Raymond and Brett as they tend the barbeque and gabble away in Afrikaans. All the cousins have disappeared to play computer games - it was ever thus. Brett, now retired, has mellowed with age and is finally realising that his youngest son is a free spirit and will never want to follow in his father's footsteps, no matter how much money he could make. Raymond is the proverbial chip off the old block, and with clipped hair neatly groomed, already looks like the successful businessman he undoubtedly is, even while wearing an apron.

"Have some salad." Eila hands me a dish of greenery. "And there's sweet potato fries for your steak on the table."

I dig my fork in the bowl and bring out some lettuce and watercress.

"Thanks. We've had such a lovely Christmas break. It'll be a shame to go back tomorrow."

Skye, a vision in pink shorts, bleached blonde hair and a scanty top despite being the wrong side of forty, speaks through a mouth full of fries.

"Why don't you all move over here and live on the estate? It's very secure here. There's plenty of space, private school for the kids, and private medical care too."

After twenty years I am pleased to be finally accepted within the family, especially by Brett, who now will never speak Afrikaans in front of me. I think deep down he is grateful that I pulled Gerrie out from the brink of his own personal abyss.

"The twins have their friends, and Gerrie has his lecturing. I have the nursery I own, and so our lives are entrenched in the UK really."

"You know you'd never need to work again if you came here." Eila looks at me earnestly. "Have a think about it."

I've often thought about it. Gerrie's opinion is that he'd rather die. I shrug my shoulders.

"One day perhaps. Who knows?"

Valerie flicks a strand of dark hair from her eyes, and takes hold of my hand.

"He'd find you wherever you are, you *know* that."

I'm momentarily lost for words, but as usual my plain-speaking sister-in-law is correct. Eila and Skye hardly ever mention Junior, but Valerie's distinct lack of tact has once again managed to shoot an arrow straight through my heart.

"He's missed out on all this, his birth right." My voice is breathy with emotion as I acknowledge my opulent surroundings. "I might even be a grandmother by now and never know it."

"That would make me a great-grandmother!" Eila tries to lighten my mood. "I'm too young yet!"

We chuckle together, but there's an empty chair at the dining table that needs to be filled. I am nearly forty years of age and half of my life is over. I do not want to go to my grave having never seen my eldest child ever again. I dread each April 10th; even after all these years it still doesn't get any better.

The twins are eager to get home; I think Jacob might have a girlfriend, but I dare not ask. He's walked a safe distance away and is talking into his phone, mumbling secretly to somebody unknown as soon as we reach Heathrow's baggage carousel. Grace waits with Gerrie for our serious amount of luggage to appear, while I yawn and feel as though I could sleep for a week.

I check my own phone. There is a message from Mum, who wonders if we are back yet. Poor Mum is coping well after Dad's death, but I know she's lonely. It seems as though my priorities are being pulled in so many different directions. I wish she would move down South, and then we could keep more of an eye on her.

I reply to Mum and then watch Grace as she sits on top of the suitcases which Gerrie has piled onto a trolley. He wheels her around in circles. They are both laughing. Her shoulder length hair flies back from her face and makes her look even more like me; she's young, carefree, and with an unblemished life to enjoy in the years ahead. I feel old before my time, weighed down with regrets and unfulfilled wishes.

Gerrie's like a big grizzly bear; nobody can nurse the blues while he's around. Jacob finishes his phone call and muscles into his sister's ride, pushing her off the trolley. Gerrie spins it until Jacob is dizzy.

"Come on." I stand up. "Are you lot going to muck about all day?"

Gerrie sends the trolley whizzing over towards me with Jacob on top of it grinning like a Cheshire cat. It's a long walk to the courtesy bus, and I'm tired. Tired as tired can be.

The Range Rover is a welcome sight, still sitting where we left it in the long stay car park. The twins climb in the back, Gerrie starts the engine, and I turn the heat up full blast.

"Are you okay?" Gerrie looks at me. "You're quiet."

I yawn.

"I hate early morning flights and cold, dreary January days."

"We'll be home before you know it." Gerrie selects reverse gear and backs out. "Close your eyes and think pleasant thoughts."

I do as instructed, and recall a young man with dark waist length hair who asked me to marry him before he even knew my name. I remember watching him strum any tune I could name, or strut about on stage with his guitar, duck-walking just like Chuck Berry. I remember with a secret smile the nights of passion in our double bed, and the look of pride and love on his face when holding his first-born son. *His. First. Born. Son.*

As much as I try to avoid these thoughts and carry on with my life, it seems that all roads lead back to the baby who was once snatched so cruelly from us.

Brett Stephen Hermann, where the hell are you?

Chapter Twenty

We're not doing too badly. Gerrie has risen to Head of

Music at the University, and I'm still happy working at the nursery, although I tend to delegate more these days. I've finally refrained from checking that each new baby we take on isn't Junior, simply because common sense tells me that he is now an adult. Gerrie and I long ago came to the conclusion that our baby was taken abroad, and sadly has grown up unaware that Ace and Maxine are not his real birth parents.

We now ensure that we focus all our energies on our twins, and try not to depress them with constant talk of Junior. Jacob is a very talented guitarist, and has joined a band at his college. Because of Gerrie's years of tuition Jake has grown up with his father's musical preferences, and can therefore play a mean rock solo. Their band sounds quite like *Nightwish* or *Evanescence*, and is complete with a stunning girl on vocals perpetually dressed in black frills a la Stevie Nicks, who all the boys are in love with, including Jake. However, Stevie reincarnated, who is actually called Mariah, doesn't seem to prefer any of them and as far as I can tell is a right little madam, playing one off against the other.

Grace is equally musical but prefers to sing in various choirs, although she hasn't yet gained enough confidence to perform solo before an audience. She has a pleasing soprano voice which could be classically trained I'm sure, but she is still young and finding her way.

If Gerrie's not playing with *Princes of Darkness*, most weekends find us driving Jake about to wherever his band, *Temptress*, is playing that night. Grace sometimes accompanies us, and it's a great way of bonding with our teenagers. I'm not sure Jake is ever too pleased to see Mum and Dad in the audience, but as we have to drive him back again it's often not worth going home and then coming out only a couple of hours' later. Gerrie stands there telling me that Chang, the drummer, is playing too fast, or that Mariah's off key, or that Ricky the bass player sucks, but he never criticises Jake. Grace enjoys the attention from youths in the mosh pits, talking to dodgy-looking characters whom you'd cross the street to avoid on a dark night.

Jake is more morose than usual as we load his guitar and amplifier into the back of the Range Rover. Gerrie swings the amp expertly into the luggage space.

"So where are we off to tonight then?"
Jake flops into the back seat beside Grace and sighs.
"*The Twist* at Colchester."
I turn around to face him from the front seat.
"Everything okay, Jake?"

"Mariah's got a new boyfriend." Grace strokes the top of Jake's hair. "Poor Jakey here is pining."

"Shut up!" Jake pushes his sister's hand away. "Just because you're a *lesbo*."

"I'm not!" Grace huffs and slides towards the opposite window. "You're better off without her anyway. She's been round the block a few too many times."

Gerrie bites his lip and starts up the engine. It's getting more like *The Carpenters* every day. Our children argue like cat and dog, but I know each twin would lay down their life for the other one.

It's about an hour's drive to Colchester. The venue doesn't look particularly salubrious from the outside, but Gerrie seems impressed with the sound system and the mixing desk as we sit at the back of the hall and watch *Temptress* setting up their equipment. However, as far as I can tell, one person seems to be missing on stage. I look at Gerrie and shout over Jake's power chords.

"Where's the lovely Mariah?"

"Who knows?" Gerrie shrugs. "Wherever she is, she'd better turn up soon."

After a while the audience begin to shuffle in and I can see Jake peeping out from backstage. Presently he runs over to us.

"Grace, you'll have to sing tonight. Mariah's sick – throwing up sick."

I turn to my daughter, who looks horrified.

"I can't!" Grace shakes her head. "No!"

Jake is not the type to take no for an answer. He pulls Grace to her feet.

"Come on, we only have to do three songs before the next band are on. We'll do the three you know the best. If you've forgotten the words, make them up as you go along; nobody will know the difference. You can sing just as well as Mariah can. *Do it for me, G!*"

His last sentence does it. My heart is in my mouth as we watch Grace take a deep breath and walk timidly on stage in her jeans and sweatshirt, looking anything *but* a temptress.

"Oh fuck." Gerrie laughs. "This'll be interesting."

Grace blinks in the spotlight as the venue's host announces the band. Somebody in the audience shouts.

"Where's Mariah?"

I watch as Jake slides nearer his sister and shouts into her microphone.

"We don't need Mariah – we've got Grace!"

He plays the opening chords of one of their songs that even *I* know the words to, having heard it so many times. To my surprise Grace launches straight in, confident, sure of herself, and with perfect pitch. The audience stop talking and listen. To say I am flabbergasted would be an understatement.

"Gerrie – she actually looks as though she's enjoying herself!"

And she is. Our daughter is a star in her torn jeans and college sweatshirt. The audience applaud loudly when the band finish their songs, and clamour for more. Gerrie claps the loudest of all.

"Be afraid Mariah, be very afraid!"

I laugh at his words. Grace looks completely at home amongst the wires and amplifiers. Her newly-washed light brown hair shines and falls over her face. Ricky and Chang are regarding her with something akin to awe. It's going to be the devil's own job to get her to go to bed later on.

Only too soon we discover the reason for Mariah's frequent bouts of vomiting. Jake drops his bombshell over dinner a few weeks' later.

"Mariah's pregnant."

"Oh?" I reply. "Who's the father?"

Grace stops eating for a moment and looks at him.

"*She* probably doesn't know, but hey, just as long as it isn't *you*."

"Another saucer of milk darling?" Jake sighs. "Her new boyfriend I suppose. I never even got to hold her hand."

Gerrie seems on the same wavelength as me, voicing what I'm already thinking.

"What's going to happen about the band then?"

Jake shrugs.

"Don't know.   I suppose we'll have to advertise for a new singer when the time comes."

"You've got one sitting next to you." I smile at Grace. "Your sister."

Grace doesn't contradict me, but waits for her brother's reply.

"I suppose Grace will be able to audition if she wants to." Jake nods. "She did a good job at *The Twist*."

I glance at Grace, who is playing it cool and trying not to appear too excited.

$\mathcal{S}$*uddenly* everybody in the family is in a band except for me. Grace gets a Saturday job frying burgers and spends her wages along the Camden Road on black lacy skirts with lots of frills, and plunging sleeveless leather bodices. Gerrie is not too keen on his princess's new look or her part-time career as a chanteuse, but in these modern days of sexual equality Grace knows he has no grounds to object. Instead, Gerrie has asked Jake to keep a watchful eye on any amorous fan who might get rather too close for his and Grace's liking.

I like these weekend family outings to gigs – standing there enjoying the music alongside people in their late teens or early twenties somehow makes me feel young again instead of being one of those invisible fortysomething mothers. I'll be quite dismayed when the twins eventually pass their driving tests and become independent. I know Gerrie enjoys it too, although the twins more often than not decline to accompany me to Gerrie's gigs. I love to see the look of pure happiness on my husband's face as he stands there posturing on stage in our local pubs and clubs with his trusty Gibson Flying V.

Chapter Twenty-One

Jake bounds into the front room after band practise as I'm catching up with 'EastEnders', my one and only vice.

"Mum, you'll never guess what?"

I pause the programme and look up smiling at my son, all six feet two inches of him.

"Okay…what?"

"Back in March Chang sent off a CD of our band to the Download Festival's Indie band competition."

Gerrie and Grace enter behind him; they're both grinning from ear to ear.

"And?" I shrug my shoulders in feigned nonchalance.

"*And*…we won the most votes from the public, so we get to play there in the Big Top in June! *Ricin* are headlining on the main stage! Awesome!"

"Wow!" I am genuinely pleased for the twins. "*Ricin*? What kind of a band name is that? I've never heard of them."

"Neither have I" Gerrie answers. "Is that because I'm an old fart?"

"Yeah." Jake nods. "But you can't help it. *Ricin* are only the best death metal band going!"

I'm pleased for the twins.

"I suppose you would be dead if you ate ricin." I chuckle. "Let's hope your gig isn't the same time as theirs then."

"It won't be." Grace puts her arms around me and gives me a kiss. "They'll be headlining on the first night. Our set is earlier in the day."

They run upstairs to talk about band business and what they're going to play and wear. I dread to think about the latter. Gerrie sinks down next to me on the sofa and yawns. I turn off EastEnders. My peace is over for the evening.

"Bit of good news for our kids, eh?"

He's tired after a long day lecturing and driving the twins to and from band practise. I snuggle up next to him.

"Download's a big deal. Is that the one where everyone wears black and all the tee-shirts are obscene?"

"That's the one." Gerrie laughs. "I'll have to lend Jake my oral sex shirt if I can find it."

"You will not!" I reply in mock indignation. "Besides – I chucked it out years ago in case the kids saw it."

"Party pooper."

"Good thing we'll be there to keep an eye on Grace." I look up at him. "I presume they'll give us backstage passes?"

Gerrie kisses the top of my head and then stands up.

"We'll see. We mustn't mollycoddle her. Jake's there; we need to step back a bit. I'm going up for a shower. What do you Brits say? I'm…knackered. It's hard work being a roadie."

"Spoken like a true Londoner, except down here they might say *cream crackered.*" I reply drily. "You need to watch EastEnders with me and pick up the lingo."

"Get ah'er mah pub!"

I laugh at his retreating back; an 'EastEnder' with a South African accent. It seems as though things are looking up for our twins.

" *How* do I look, Mum?"

I'm frankly appalled at the sight of my daughter standing there in thigh length black divers' boots, fishnet tights, miniscule black shorts, and her favourite leather bodice. Her straightened hair is parted in the middle and falls either side of her face like two dark curtains. I dread to think what Gerrie's reaction is going to be.

"How much are you going to charge your punters?"

"Mum!" Grace appears crestfallen. "Be serious!"

"I am." I nod. "You look like you're on the game. Your father's going to have an epi when he catches sight of you."

"He won't until I'm on the stage." Grace replies rather too firmly. "It's Download. I can hardly wear a twin set and pearls."

"Well at least wear that frilly black skirt you've got." I sigh. "I think you've gone a bit over the top."

Grace pouts.

"I bet you don't care what Jake's wearing. He's got a tee-shirt that says *I'm not a gynaecologist, but I'll have a look.*"

I cannot help but laugh. It breaks the tension, as Grace joins in.

"*See*! It's alright for *him*."

I shrug.

"We're just looking out for you, Grace. Tell me you're not going to walk around the festival site with that outfit on."

"I'll take the skirt for that." Grace replies. "Just don't tell Dad...*please*."

I hold up my hands in mock surrender.

"Alright, but you'll be for it …you know what he's like."

Grace gives me a hug.

"I'll take that risk. Thanks Mum."

We hit the M1 at 9am on a baking June day. I've insisted on getting hotel rooms for Grace and I for the 3 day festival, as I do not envisage getting much sleep on the hard ground surrounded by hundreds of inebriated festival goers. Gerrie and Jake are of course revelling in the chance to let their hair down, so to speak, and become part of the great unwashed in our two-man tent. I need Gerrie there to keep an eye on Jake. After losing one child I cannot bear the thought that Jake might 'overdo' things to keep up with Chang and Ricky and drink himself into oblivion, even choking to death on his own vomit like John Henry Bonham had done back in 1980.

The Range Rover eats up the 120 miles effortlessly. We join the long tailback a couple of miles from the festival site, and Gerrie turns up the air conditioning, leans back and stretches.

"I envy you girls in a hotel room tonight."

"No you don't." I laugh. "You and Jake will be peeing up a fence with the best of them."

Grace pulls face.

"Ugh, gross."

"As if I would." Jake gives Grace a playful punch. "I'll be queueing for half an hour to pee in fetid festibogs instead."

Jake checks his phone messages.

"Artists have got a different entrance." He announces. "Chang's already here. He says our one is before the main entrance. I'll look out for it. Dad, you'd better put the pass on the dashboard."

Jake can hardly contain his excitement. Grace seems quite calm. I hope for her sake and Gerrie's blood pressure that she has packed her calf length skirt.

Chapter Twenty-Two

The twins are ensconced backstage, leaving Gerrie and me to walk around the site. It's blazing hot and there doesn't seem to be much shade. Creatures-from-the-deep dressed in black and sporting many piercings and chains growl on stage, while guitarists fill the air with deafening power chords.

The place looks like a landfill site already, with paper plates full of half-eaten food thrown on the grass, which is still soggy from recent rainfall. Empty polystyrene cups that had once held beer lie strewn about. Young boys run around picking up as many cups as they can manage, piling them one on top of the other to make huge towers before returning them to the bar for a small payment. Gerrie chuckles at the sight of two youngsters racing towards the same cup.

"Jake will be doing the cup dash tomorrow, mark my words."

"If he hasn't got a post-gig hangover." I reply. "For God's sake keep an eye on him tonight."

Gerrie points and laughs at a man in a kilt with the back of it tucked into his belt, showing a bare backside.

"It's good for boys to let off steam."

"Nice little bum." I cannot help but notice. "You should get one of those."

"I've already got a nice little bum."

Gerrie puts his arm around my shoulders and we meander past stalls selling black tee-shirts with motifs that I could never show to Eila or my mother. I laugh as I see a notice hanging outside one of the bars near the Big Top.

"We've got to show proof that we're over eighteen if we want a beer."

"Show them your wrinkles."

"Hey!" I give Gerrie a playful punch. "Cheeky! Have you looked at yourself recently?"

"I have." He nods. "I look just like my bloody father."

I scrutinise his face, noticing the inevitable laughter lines around his eyes and mouth that have appeared in recent years.

"Not with that stubble and long hair you don't. Come on, let's get a beer before the band go on stage."

There's a bit of a queue, but it's nice to hide from the merciless sun for a while under the marquee's canvas cover. Beer or cider are the only two choices available. I plump for a cup of cider and sink down on the grass outside.

"I'll never drink all of this. I'll be legless."

"What a shame." Gerrie takes a large swig of beer. "I'll have to finish it off."

We sit in companionable silence and watch the festival-goers wandering to and fro. From the Big Top comes a deep roar from the audience as a band begins to play. The sun beats down on my forehead. I fish a baseball cap out of my rucksack and check the line-up on my programme.

"We've got another couple of hours before our kids are on, enough time to get something to eat."

Gerrie chuckles.

"If you can find something amongst the buggered burgers and other shit. I know what you're like."

I point to a food outlet opposite.

"I fancy one of those industrial sized Yorkshire puddings with sausages and mash."

"Just as long as you're not chucking up all night like you were a couple of years' ago at the Isle of Wight."

"That chicken wrap was off – it must have been." I take a sip of cider. "I'll be alright as long as the bangers aren't pink inside."

I turn and lean my back against Gerrie's. The warmth from his body mingles unpleasantly with the heat from the sun above. I reach one hand up his back.

"Ugh, your tee-shirt is all damp."

There is no reply and I know he's got his eyes closed. The band in the Big Top is causing the audience to become quite vociferous in their appreciation. I just hope our kids receive the same adulation.

My heart is in my mouth as we walk into the Big Top twenty minutes before *Temptress* is due to begin their set. I see only a few people about. I don't know if they're sheltering from the heat or curious to find out more about the unknown band who are lucky enough to have won Download's competition. Chang is tuning his drums, and Jake and Ricky have plugged in their guitars and are warming up their fingers on the frets. There is no sign of Grace.

I wave to Jake, but he's off in his own little world.

"Leave him." Gerrie states firmly. "He won't know we're here."

One of the organisers ambles up onto the stage and announces the band to a muted applause. A few more people stroll into the Big Top. Jake power-chords an introduction to *Temptress's* first song, which brings a crowd of teenagers running up to stand by us at the front. I wait for the inevitable bombshell as Grace slinks out towards the microphone.

"What the *fuck*!" Gerrie turns to face me. "Did you know she was wearing *that*?"

I shrug my shoulders and grimace in mock horror.

"It's a new one on me."

Our daughter has jettisoned her black frilly skirt in favour of the contentious shorts, fishnet tights, leather bodice, and thigh length boots. There are loud catcalls from a group of young men somewhere to our rear. Raucous festival goers clutching cups of beer pour in to the Big Top and voice their approval of Grace's attire. Gerrie's face turns a kind of apoplexic purple.

"I'm going to have a word with that young lady!"

I put an arm around his waist and give him a squeeze.

"Leave her, Gerrie. Look how confident she is!"

Grace is radiant, basking in the unexpected adulation. Her voice rings loud and true, in perfect pitch. More festival goers pile in until I start to feel rather claustrophobic. However, I am determined not going to miss a single note of the performance. It appears that our daughter has indeed become a temptress, just for a short while.

Every song ends in loud cheers and applause, bringing yet more people into the Big Top until I begin to feel a kind of unwanted pressure from the hundreds of bodies. However, Gerrie knows what I'm like and stands behind me with his arms around my waist, making me feel somewhat safer.

There are shouts for more, but I rather think that *Temptress* have run out of songs. Grace confers with Jake and the others at the end of their set while the audience stamp their feet impatiently. Finally she runs back to the microphone.

"We're going to sing the first song again!"

I take a quick look behind me. All eyes are focused on my daughter, who has the crowd in the palm of her hand. The stamping ceases, Jake's guitar makes my ears burn, and to my horror a mosh pit forms to my right. About twenty hirsute and slightly inebriated festival goers clad in black begin to head-bang in time with the rhythm section. There is nowhere for me to move to as they run madly around in circles holding aloft plastic severed heads on sticks, brushing my right side as Gerrie moves in-between them and myself and shouts in my ear.

"The song will finish in a minute. One of the organisers is already at the side of the stage!"

I close my eyes and try to project my thoughts away to an empty beach full of palm trees and white sand, where I sit serenely with Gerrie and sip nectar from a coconut shell.

Cheering and applause are deafening as the song comes to an end, which bring me out of my reverie. The announcer gives out some information regarding the next band, but nobody is listening. Our twins stand there in the limelight, stunned at the audience's reaction. Chang and Ricky grin at each other as they move over to Jake and Grace and envelop them in a bear hug before waving to the crowd. Then all four jump up and down like demented punk rockers on pogo sticks. Jake suddenly remembers that we're in the front row and runs over to us. He's sweaty and deliriously happy.

"Awesome, eh?"

Gerrie nods and shakes his hand.

"Fantastic!"

I can only agree, but by then the next band are on stage and wanting to set up their equipment. As the members of *Temptress* come down to earth and begin to quickly dismantle their instruments, a phrase comes to mind that my mother always drummed into me:

After the Lord Mayor's show comes the dustcart.

Chapter Twenty-Three

The pair of them are still riding high when we meet up for dinner. Thankfully Grace has exchanged the short shorts for a more acceptable calf-length gypsy skirt, and to my amusement we have to stop several times on the way to the hot food kiosks in order for the twins to sign programmes from people who had seen them perform earlier on. I tease Grace as a young man thrusts a programme in her face.

"You're famous!"

"She's getting more requests than me because of those shorts." Jake watches his sister with a twinge of envy. "Perhaps *I* ought to do the same next time."

"Nobody's going to wear those shorts ever again." Gerrie gives the youth a stare as he walks off. "Not you, and definitely not Grace."

"Dad!" Grace makes a face. "Don't be such a spoilsport!"

I take Grace's arm and lead her up to a man selling hot jacket potatoes.

"Come on, let's choose our filling and get a spud."

The boys are more inclined towards burgers and chips, and I'm just happy to have avoided the usual father/daughter World War Three about what she chooses to wear. Grace and I clutch our plastic forks and polystyrene containers of potatoes and baked beans, and wander off to find an unadulterated patch of grass. I sink down and adjust a wide sunhat to shade my eyes from the sun's merciless glare. I raise a forkful of beans to my lips

"Dad's only worried about what some guy might do if he's fixated on your shorts."

I watch Grace roll her eyes in that oh-so-irritating-way that she's had since she was a child of five.

"How can he do anything if I'm on the stage?"

"There's always after the show." I chew and talk at the same time. "He could follow you out the stage door."

"Mum. If I think *what if* every time then I'd never do anything."

Her voice drops as though she is trying to reason with an imbecile. I suppose she has a point. I come to the swift conclusion that it's hard work being the mother of a teenage girl.

The twins wander off for the rest of the day with Chang and

Ricky, leaving Gerrie and me to sit on the grass in the cooling air and listen to the early evening bands. Gerrie lies down on our rug and puts a recently purchased cowboy hat over his eyes.

"I'm knackered. Look out for the piss-in-a-bottle-and-fling-it brigade. Wake me up when *Ricin* come on."

"I'm sure you'll hear them." I chuckle. "They're not exactly shrinking violets. What piss-in-a-bottle-brigade?"

Pretty soon I can hear even breathing and the odd gentle snore. I feel like joining my husband in the Land of Nod, but do not trust the groups of vociferous young men clad in black *Ricin* tee-shirts who are slowly but surely filling in all the gaps in the assembled crowd and sending plastic bottles filled with dubious coloured liquids flying through the air.

As the evening air cools, families pack up rugs or foldaway chairs and stand up, ready for the headline band's much awaited appearance. Gerrie hauls himself upright and goes off to buy a couple of beers. I pick up my phone and dial Grace's number; she shouts into my ear straight away.

"I'm still alive, Mum!"

I laugh.

"Glad to hear it. Just wanted to let you know that *Ricin* will be on soon."

"Yeah, I know; we're right down the front!"

I focus my gaze past many people waving colourful flags on willowy plastic poles to the seething mass of bodies in front of the stage and give a slight shudder.

"We're over at the back near the Rock Bar if it gets too much."

"Nah! We're okay! It stinks a bit iffy down here though, but see ya later!"

Quite how anybody could enjoy the claustrophobic conditions down at the front is beyond me, where it also seems that the majority of the piss-in-a-bottle brigade like to aim their bodily fluids at. I'm happy to be somewhere near the back and watch the band perform on one of the two enormous screens now being erected either side of the stage.

There's a definite buzz in the air by the time Gerrie returns with our drinks. He hands me a cup, and I thankfully take a few sips of lager.

"Time to pack up our stuff." I stand, roll up our rug, and put it in the rucksack. "There's no room to sit down anymore."

Bodily fluids flung, groups of youths begin chanting. I look at Gerrie, puzzled.

"What are they saying?"

Gerrie laughs.

"They're shouting for Ear, Noise, and Throat, the three members of *Ricin*. I've heard them on CDs but never seen them live. I'm looking forward to it."

The two TV screens spring into life, the sun sinks lower over the top of the stage, and Ricin's logo appears on view to great applause and cheering from the crowd.

On screen there now comes a short interview backstage with *Ricin's* band members to whet our appetites; first off is drummer *Ear*, who mumbles unintelligible responses to the interviewer's questions whilst tapping his drum sticks against a table. I have no idea as to the questions or his answers due to the roar of the audience on seeing one of their idols. *Noise* brandishes an expensive looking guitar and makes V signs with the fingers of his right hand, but again as far as I'm concerned he might have been speaking Swahili.

I only really take notice when singer and bass player *Throat* appears and sits down next to the other two, causing the most deafening roar to erupt from the crowd that I've ever heard in my life. My legs suddenly feel weak and I clutch Gerrie for support. He's concentrating on texting Jake, and looks down at me in surprise.

"What's the matter?"

"Look up at the screen!" My voice is barely audible. "Who do you see?"

I pinch myself to make sure that the spitting image of Gerrie as he was twenty years' ago is not a dream and is actually on view for everyone to see, right down to the waist length hair, the shape of his face and even the dimple on his chin. There is no mistake. *Throat* is none other than Brett Stephen Hermann in person; my Junior – my baby. Gerrie takes a deep, shaky breath, hardly able to believe his eyes.

"Fuck!"

In a broad Australian accent *Throat* goes on to thank his parents, who just so happen to be backstage, for all they have done for him. To my horror the camera pans behind and to the side where Ace and Maxine, now somewhat older and greyer, smile proudly at the camera.

Chapter Twenty-Four

Gerrie hauls the rucksack on his back and takes hold of my hand.

"Come on!"

He pulls me along behind him as he elbows his way through a chanting crowd towards where a row of security men guard a large area designated for the press which is roped off at the front of the stage. I shout over the general clamour while keeping my eyes fixed firmly on the screen, not wanting to miss a moment of our son's interview.

"They'll never let us backstage!"

"I'm going to find Jake and Grace!" Gerrie scans the audience as he edges ever forwards. "They've got passes. They might be able to get us in!"

We get as near to the front as we can, without starting a riot. Gerrie dials Jake's number and puts the phone to his ear.

"Ah, nothing!" He sighs in exasperation. "He's probably shouting his lungs out with all the rest of them."

The interview finishes and still stunned, I look around. The audience is too densely packed for me to pick out the twins, and all I want to do is get to where I can feel free without somebody breathing down the back of my neck. I nudge Gerrie and point towards the front hoardings where a closed door I assume leads to the backstage area is guarded by a proverbial brick shit-house of a man clad in black.

"I'm going over there!"

"Okay!" Gerrie yells in my ear. "Wait near the Neanderthal and I'll search round for the twins! I'll catch up with you in a minute!"

Neanderthal gives me the once over as I reach the edge of the crowd. I decide to stand far enough away from him so that Gerrie can see me but at the same time still be able to get a decent view of the front part of the stage, where to my delight I can now see my son strutting confidently up to the microphone and raising one fist in the air.

"Hello Download!"

There is a roar of approval accompanied by deafening power chords and an amplified kick drum that causes my chest to vibrate. Junior's hair, the same brown as Gerrie's, blows out behind him from an industrial fan situated somewhere down near the front monitors. He wears chains, combat trousers, and a black tee-shirt slashed with holes carrying the motif 'Aussies do it better'. He has the audience in the palm of his hand.

"Let's fuckin' rock!"

I am mesmerised as my son bends forwards, bass guitar swinging, and begins to mosh to the rhythm, along with the hundreds of fans in front of him. From my vantage point I can now see an older looking woman with short salt-and-pepper hair that was obviously once ginger standing in the wings at the side of the stage watching the show, who is wearing what I imagine to be an Access-All-Areas pass.

Maxine.

Hot stabs of uncontrolled anger course through me as I kill her a thousand times with an imaginary shotgun. However, she is still smiling and has her gaze fixed on Junior as he growls out unintelligible words in that creature-of-the-deep way just like Ace used to do.

White hot rage sends me storming over to Neanderthal man who shoots me an evil eye as I approach. My brain is firing on all cylinders and racing ahead to find the right way to gain his sympathy.

"Excuse me." I can only attempt a half smile in my present state. "My son's band played in the Big Top this afternoon."

There is no indication that any of my words are reaching the depths of his being. I carry on regardless.

"Does his pass allow backstage access to the main stage?"

Neanderthal silently shakes his head and continues to block the doorway. I quickly arrive at the conclusion it would be pointless to pursue the matter any further. The frustration that only a makeshift doorway separates me from my son causes me to have to wipe away a stab of tears, which I do as Gerrie hurries towards me from the direction of the front-of-stage moshpit accompanied by Jake and Grace.

"I found them!" Gerrie waves at me. "They've still got their passes!"

A struggle through the moshpit has made him sweat. Jake, dishevelled and disgruntled, appears less than pleased at being dragged away from his favourite band, and looks back over his shoulder at the stage. Grace, equally out of sorts, smooths down some ruffled strands of hair.

"What's this all about, Dad?"

I interrupt and shake my head.

"It's no use, Gerrie. Neanderthal won't let us in. I've already asked him."

"In where?" Jake shouts a reply with one eye on the stage. "What are you talking about?"

"Don't shout, Jake." I admonish my son in a strained voice. "What I'm talking about is this." I point to the stage. "See that singer from Ricin over there, and how much he looks like Dad? Well… he's your brother, the baby that was stolen from us all those years ago."

Both twins stare at me with their mouths open.

"But he can't be!" Jake looks at the stage and then back at me. "His name isn't Brett or Junior, it's Leigh. He's called Leigh Havilland and he's Australian!"

"Nevertheless, he is Brett." I am still firm in my conviction. "I recognise the woman in the wings at the side of the stage. She's the one I gave him to, to temporarily to look after for just one week. Besides – look at him. He's the image of Dad when he was younger."

"Oh my God!" Grace stares at the stage. "You're right, Mum! That old photo of Dad and his guitar in the front room…it's Leigh Havilland! Until you mentioned it I've never given it a thought!"

"Jeez!" Jake sits down suddenly on the grass. "He's my *brother*?"

I nod.

"He sure is, but there's no way we can get backstage without the right pass."

Gerrie dials a number on his phone.

"I'm going to speak to the police. We mustn't let them get away. I know she's probably retired now, but what was the name of that policewoman who handled our case?"

I have instant recall on anything to do with Junior.

"Judith Farrow."

He wanders away from the amplifiers while I stand with Jake and Grace and watch mesmerised as our eldest son controls seventy five thousand people with the greatest of ease. Maxine is enjoying herself. The twins and I are still rooted to the spot with disbelief as Gerrie runs up behind us.

"Apparently there's a police station on site. We need to go back near the entrance – that's where they hang out. Come on!"

He grabs my fingers with one hand and Grace's arm with the other. Jake leads the way, and the four of us push through the crowd that stretches to the food kiosks at the rear of the arena. Jake is like a wild thing, elbowing and shoving people out of the way. I am scared one of them might fight back and swing a punch.

"Stop pushing, Jake!" I yell as I run. "Somebody's going to hit you in a minute!"

The police station is to the right of the entrance, and we make it in record time. We're all puffing and panting as Jake throws open the door.

"You've got to help us!"

Three uniformed officers are eating burgers and chips. All of them look up surprised, in mid-chew. It's now or never; if they don't go for our story it's my belief that we'll probably never see Junior ever again.

Chapter Twenty-Five

"*What* can I do for you?"

One officer puts down his burger and stands up.

My legs feel shaky with adrenaline and unaccustomed sprinting. I sink down slowly onto a nearby chair.

"Our eldest son was snatched from us when he was a baby by the woman who is watching him from the side of the main stage." I sigh and hope against hope I do not sound like a madwoman. "There'll be old case records of his disappearance I'm sure. The officer who dealt with our case was a Judith Farrow."

All three policeman are listening intently as I gabble on. Gerrie, Jake and Grace seem to have been suddenly struck mute.

"When I saw him on stage, how much he resembles my husband, and then the woman standing watching him in the wings, I realised straight away that Leigh Havilland is our son whom we named Brett Stephen Hermann, or Junior for short."

To my relief Gerrie finds his voice.

"The day Junior went missing, I took a picture of that woman who's on the side of the stage now as she held our baby. We've never seen either of them since until this day."

With a start of surprise I remember the photo of a serious-looking Maxine standing in our hallway holding Junior quite awkwardly, which Gerrie had stuck in the one album that I could hardly ever bear to peruse.

"When *Ricin's* set finishes, they'll be away." Gerrie continues firmly. "You'll need to detain Leigh Havilland and the woman, Maxine, who is posing as his mother. We need to be reunited with our son, but we haven't got the right passes to gain access backstage."

"Ask Maxine to have an MRI scan of her abdomen." I add in triumph. "She can't possibly be his mother, as I know for a fact that she was born without a womb."

I have a feeling the three officers have never come across a problem like this before. The one already standing up speaks first.

"We'll call some backup and check out your story. I'm PC Eversleigh by the way. Please give me your names and address, and the address where the baby was taken from. I'll make a call to the main station and they can get the old records pulled up."

I listen to *Ricin* blasting away in the background as Gerrie gives the policemen our details. Jake and Grace are already half out of the door and watching the stage in a kind of enraptured awe.

"That's our brother out there!"

Jake grins at Grace, who nods and shivers.

By the time *Ricin* are into their encore things start to move

on a bit. Backup arrives in the shape of three more policemen and we follow them rather more sedately this time through the crowd, who are now waving glowing cigarette lighters against the rapidly darkening evening. Neanderthal is still steadfast at his post, and looks surprised as the policemen arrive with the four of us following behind. To my great joy after a brief conversation he heaves his bulk to one side and lets us pass through the hallowed portal.

The first person I see is a balding Ace, who is sitting on a flight case and strumming an acoustic guitar, totally oblivious to his surroundings. Gerrie lets out an expletive and begins to run towards him, overtaking the police. Panicked at the thought of what he might do, I yell at the top of my voice.

"No! Gerrie – stop!"

My words are swallowed up by *Ricin's* powerful amplifiers. Gerrie reaches Ace and punches him completely off the flight case. His guitar whizzes through the air and crash lands on the grass several feet away. The police and Jake reach Gerrie within seconds and hold him in a firm grip. Grace clings to me like a limpet while I listen to Gerrie's words as his mouth spits out venom in Ace's direction, who is now sporting a split lip and lying on the ground.

"You fucking bastard!"

Ace's eyes tell me that straight away he has sized up the situation. He gets to his feet with difficulty, wiping his mouth with the back of his hand. He doesn't look very well, and has gained about four stones in weight in the intervening years and is obviously not as agile as he once was. He remains silent while Gerrie struggles to free himself, all the while hurling more insults at Ace, who stands there looking at us with a stunned expression.

"That fucker stole our baby!"

A roving reporter wearing a 'Press' lanyard who is eager to catch the first shots of *Ricin* backstage begins to snap photos. Over a cheering crowd I can hear Junior announcing *Ricin's* last song and thanking his father, whom he calls up to join him on stage. The whole scenario is absolutely surreal. Gerrie calms down, shakes himself free, and panting, points a finger to his erstwhile bandmate.

"You're dead, mate!"

To my utter surprise, Ace looks away from Gerrie, raises the palms of his hands, and addresses the police, while the reporter looks on.

"I don't know who this man is, but he needs arresting. Please get him out of here, whoever he is. I'll certainly be pressing charges of assault and threatening behaviour. My name is Robert Havilland and my wife's name is Nancy. We are Australian citizens and have never been to the UK before. Now my son is calling me onto the stage for their last song, so I've got to go."

There is a very mild Australian twang to his words. I double check his features, but there is no doubt in my mind who he is. Ace grabs his guitar and makes a run for the door at the back of the stage, disappearing from view through a line of security guards. Gerrie and Jake start out after Ace with the police in hot pursuit, but they are held back at the entrance by several guards.

"His name is Ace!" I run forward towards the police. "We entrusted our baby to this man and his partner for one week only, nineteen years' ago!" I want to cry in frustration but take a deep breath before continuing. "The baby is Leigh Havilland who is now performing on stage, although he was born Brett Stephen Hermann. His partner is standing there watching our son – her name is Maxine. They stole our baby and took him to live in Australia!"

Grace catches up with me and we cling together. Gerrie sinks to the ground, spent. Jake squats down and puts his arms around Gerrie's neck. The policemen confer and then one of them makes a brief phone call before speaking.

"My colleague DI Lambert here will take you all to the main station in town, and we'll call for backup to bring Mr and Mrs Havilland along after the show, as we'll have to stay here. Leigh Havilland will need to join us with members from his security team, as word will get out somehow to the fans. There's obviously a situation here that needs sorting out."

"Too bloody right it does." Gerrie nods, gives Jake's arm a squeeze, and gets to his feet. "It's time for our son to know his real parents."

The reporter, who up until now has been an interested onlooker, holds up his hand and speaks to me."

"I'm Mike Prentiss from The Daily Trouper. I'm doing a quick after-show interview with Leigh Havilland for our newspaper. Would you and your husband like to tell us your story? We pay well for an exclusive."

"Absolutely." I nod energetically. "You just say when and where."

"Here's my details." Mike Prentiss thrusts a business card into my hand. "Call me tomorrow."

There's a massive cheer from the audience as *Ricin's* last song comes to an end. The two policemen wait for Ace, Maxine and the band to come off stage, while Gerrie, Jake, Grace and I are led out through a VIP exit to a waiting patrol car.

Chapter Twenty-Six

It's heart-breaking as Gerrie, Jake, Grace and I sit opposite

Ace, Maxine and Junior at the police station. Junior, freshly showered and wearing a black tee shirt and clean-looking jeans, regards Gerrie and I with utter contempt after checking the time on a designer watch strapped to his wrist.

"How long have I got to stay here?"

DI Lambert shrugs and sends a quick glance to a colleague sitting next to him at the formica-covered table.

"Until we've established exactly what is going on, I expect. I shall be taping this interview." He switches on a voice recorder before carrying on. "For the record there is myself, DI Lambert, together with PC Green. The date is Friday June the ninth, two thousand and seventeen and the time is twenty three hundred hours. We have Mr and Mrs Havilland and Leigh Havilland, together with Mr and Mrs Hermann and their two children Jake and Grace."

I'm tired and want it all to end. Junior is fidgety, obviously still full of adrenaline. Ace and Maxine glare at us across the table. Gerrie puts his hands behind his head and stares them both out. DI Lambert clears his throat.

"Mrs Hermann, perhaps you'd like to start."

All eyes are fixed on me and I don't know where to start. I look at Gerrie and am suddenly buoyed by his smile and his nearness. I decide it's time for me to fight for my son.

"I had a baby boy on April the tenth nineteen ninety eight. We called him Brett Stephen after his grandfather, to be known as Junior." I want to cry as I look at Junior's blank stare. "His father, Gerrie, is a musician and at that time he played guitar in a band called *Thrash*, with Ace, the same man over there who now calls himself Robert Havilland. His girlfriend at the time was Maxine, who is now calling herself Nancy Havilland."

Ace shakes his head and Junior begins to tap irritatingly on the table with his fingers. I ignore both of them and carry on.

"*Thrash* had the chance to make it big, but they needed forty thousand pounds to support and tour for a month with *Death Throes*, a heavy metal band who were famous at that time. There was a deadline to pay the money."

At the mention of *Death Throes*, Junior looks up at me and then at Gerrie. His eyes scan Gerrie's face. I hope against hope he is noticing the resemblance. I carry on blindly.

"Gerrie's parents are very wealthy and live in South Africa, but they wanted him to go home and follow in the family's diamond business. Gerrie didn't want to – he wanted to be a rock star just like Leigh Havilland is now. After he married me in order to stay in the UK his father disapproved and stopped paying him any allowance. We had to work or starve."

I see Maxine smile proudly at Junior, who returns her smile with one of his own. I want to rip off her head.

"We came up with a plan that Ace and Maxine would take Junior off to a caravan in Felixstowe and hide him there for a week. We would invent some kidnappers who were asking for forty five thousand pounds ransom money – we were going to pay five thousand pounds to Ace and Maxine. We were certain that Gerrie's father would pay when it came to the crunch. However, he didn't come up with the money for weeks until well after the deadline to pay *Death Throes* and Gerrie and the band lost their chance to hit the big time, but Junior ended up *really* being kidnapped by those two." I point to Ace and Maxine. "Ace and Maxine never returned our baby and instead disappeared with him, and by the sound of his accent they went to Australia."

Both Ace and Maxine are shaking their heads now. Junior is sitting up straighter and has stopped tapping. I add another thought that has suddenly popped into my head.

"Maxine told me at the time that she had been born without a womb and couldn't have children. I suppose she decided to grab at the chance of being a mother because childlessness had made her desperate." I send Maxine a shooting stab of anger by way of a glare. "There are two ways to prove what I'm saying – for Maxine to have an MRI scan of her abdomen and also for all of us to undergo DNA testing."

"It's all lies!" Maxine points a shaking finger in my direction. "You're fucking mad! We want to press charges!"

She is getting rattled and I'm pleased that my words are having some effect. DI Lambert turns his gaze away from me and towards Ace and Maxine.

"Now let's have your story."

Ace licks his lips nervously.

"Our story is that we've lived in Australia all our lives and that we've never been to the UK, so how could we have kidnapped their baby?"

Maxine nods in agreement.

"It's all a pack of lies. Leigh needs to get back to his after-show party. We're invited to it too, and we're missing out."

"Tough shit." Gerrie gives Maxine a smile that doesn't quite reach his eyes. "I agree to DNA testing, and if you don't I want to know why."

Maxine tosses what is left of her once flame-coloured hair.

"Why should I, just because *you* want me to?"

"I don't agree." Ace shakes his head. "We've done nothing wrong and I object to being treated like a criminal."

"Just do it, Dad." Junior pipes up and looks at his watch again. "Afterwards we can get out of here. I agree to be tested if it'll speed things up."

DI Lambert nods as Ace and Maxine silently fume at Junior's decision. Jake and Grace look at each other and speak as one.

"We want to be tested too."

I grin at them.

"So do I."

After swabs are taken for testing, we are free to go. Ace, Maxine and Junior are driven back to the Download site, where Junior is allowed to carry on with his UK tour. However, Ace and Maxine are instructed to give their passports to the festival police, and to my joy are now not allowed to leave the country but must stay in a nearby hotel until further notice. Gerrie, Jake, Grace and I give Mike Prentiss his eagerly awaited interview the following day, and then return home to await the results of the tests. As soon as we unlock the front door, Jake receives a phone call from Chang to say that *Temptress* now have a manager.

Chapter Twenty-Seven

I can hardly contain my excitement as Gerrie and I together with Jake and Grace in the back seat drive back up the M1 to meet DI Lambert at an appointed time for the DNA test results. I'm on a strange kind of high, which is tinged with a fair amount of sadness. I realise our eldest son will never consider us as his parents, and was too young at the time to have had any recollection of us at all. I burn with righteous injustice at the mental picture of Maxine waiting proudly in the wings on the Download stage.

"She's having the life that should have been mine."

Gerrie changes into sixth gear and shrugs.

"Don't let it eat you up. The test results will show who's telling the truth. With a bit of luck you'll be able to visit them in prison and gloat."

The twins tap away on their phones, happy to have missed a day at college, and are oblivious to my mood. I look out of the window and let the years roll by; Junior wearing his blue Babygro and the white cardigan I was so pleased with because it was my first effort at knitting. The night feeds in those hectic two weeks after the birth where it seemed the whole world slept except Gerrie and me. The pride I felt as I pushed Junior in the pram to the supermarket where I had worked to show him off.

We'd had so little time with our newborn baby. I want to leap with joy now that we've found our son, but I feel a sudden need to cry a great river of tears.

"Let them rot." I shake my head. "They'll get no visits from me."

The police station is bathed in late June sunlight as Gerrie pulls up on the gravel forecourt. Jake stops texting and leans forward.

"Mum, Malcolm Wainwright's got us a gig at the O2 Academy at Islington in September."

I turn around to face him.

"Who's Malcolm Wainwright when he's at home?"

"Our manager." Grace pipes up. "We told you – remember?"

I feel a pang of guilt at forgetting that the twins were celebrating with their own good news. I ruffle Jake's hair and smile at him.

"That's great! Dad and I will be in the front row for sure."

"We need a van for all the gear." Jake looks at Gerrie. "Dad, can you get us one and drive it?"

Gerrie turns off the engine and yawns.

"So I'm a roadie now, am I? I assume Malcolm, whoever he is, will be paying for it?"

"Well…"

Jake's voice trails off, disappointed. Gerrie opens the driver's door and laughs.

"Course I will son, if it's going to help you out."

"Thanks!"

Jake leaps out of the back seat, closely followed by Grace. I wish to God I had some of their *joie de vivre*. I catch up with the twins and Gerrie and we walk through into the now familiar reception area, where a miserable looking couple with three children sit silently on a bench. I throw them a half smile as we make our way up to the desk. Gerrie addresses the clerk on duty as I take a quick look over my shoulder to see if I can spot Ace and Maxine. However, the rest of the waiting area is empty.

"Mr and Mrs Hermann. We have an appointment with DI Lambert."

We are shown into the same interview room as before, where DI Lambert is already seated and leafing through a sheaf of papers. He stands up as we enter.

"Come in! Please take a seat. I have the results of the DNA tests here."

My heart begins to beat a whole lot faster. The policeman looks at his watch.

"Mr and Mrs Havilland should be here any minute now, and so we'll wait. We requested that Leigh accompanies them, and so I hope he does as of course he is an innocent party in all of this and we cannot force him to attend."

Eleven o'clock has rolled on to eleven forty and two cups of tea by the time we hear footsteps outside. The door opens to reveal Junior wearing mirrored sunglasses, a Bruce Willis type white vest before all the shooting started, plus the usual jeans and baseball cap. He's flanked by what I can only assume are two minders, judging by the size of their biceps. His dark hair hangs loose down his back, and he is the epitome of what a rock star should look like. I nudge the twins to close their mouths, which are hanging open in awe. He glances towards DI Lambert.

"I got your message. I can't get Mum and Dad on the phone though. Don't know where they are."

Junior plonks himself down on a vacant chair, and the heavies move to the back of the room and stand like statues. I cannot take my eyes from his features, which are so like Gerrie's. He stares me out, obviously irritated.

"Had a good look?"

He is arrogant and sure of himself, and the Australian twang is so foreign on a child of mine. I feel my face flushing and turn away. DI Lambert stands up and walks to the door to the interview room, where he speaks briefly to somebody unseen before returning.

"Let's begin." He takes his seat again and addresses Junior. "I've sent somebody to your parents' hotel room to check on their whereabouts. However, I must inform you that according to the evidence I have here, your DNA matches ninety nine point nine percent with that of Mr and Mrs Hermann and their two children. They may have brought you up, but there is no way that Robert and Nancy Havilland can be your birth parents. My two colleagues who are now on the way to their hotel have instructions to arrest them for unlawful kidnapping and to take DNA samples as further proof."

The relief is overwhelming. Junior appears as stunned as the rest of us. Gerrie gets to his feet and leans over towards Junior, offering him an outstretched hand.

"Welcome home, son."

The reunion isn't quite how I had imagined it would be. My baby is a man; his personality has been formed by Ace and Maxine and by life experiences which I have not been privy to. His name isn't Brett Hermann – it's Leigh Havilland. I have to stop calling him *Junior*. Leigh looks from Gerrie to me and then to the twins.

"So … now we have to walk off into the sunset and play happy families?"

His fingers tap out a tune on the table. I feel a raging disappointment but decide to say my piece and to hell with it.

"It's up to you." I reply in the same offhand manner. "We won't crowd you or expect anything from you. However, we'd like to keep in touch if you're willing. You were taken from us as a newborn, and we've waited such a long time to see you again."

Jake points to Grace before speaking to the brother he's never known.

"We're in a band too. Our manager's just got us a gig at the O2 Academy in Islington. Perhaps you'd like to come and see us play?"

"Huh, I don't think so." Leigh sighs. "Thanks for the offer though."

There is an awkward silence, broken by DI Lambert's mobile phone ringing. After a brief conversation, he ends the call and looks at us.

"Nancy and Robert Havilland have disappeared – apparently they checked out late last night. We still have their passports though, so they cannot leave the country."

"Oh yes they can." Gerrie nods. "And they probably have done by now. It's my guess they've kept their UK passports in their real names up to date. We did tell you that Robert and Nancy Havilland are aliases, but I don't know what their real names are other than Ace and Maxine."

Leigh looks at Gerrie in disgust.

"So what does that make *me*?"

Gerrie shrugs.

"It makes you my son and the brother to Jake and Grace here, but I expect you can call yourself what you like, although I'd tend to call you an arrogant bastard."

Gerrie's short fuse has just detonated, and I hear Grace take a sharp intake of breath. I am crushed beyond belief at the outcome of the meeting which I had imagined in my head for years, and am finding it hard to control the tears which threaten to stream down my face. I notice the muscles in Leigh's jaw twitching, just like Gerrie's are. Our son is the absolute image of his father.

"Sorry." Leigh sighs. "I haven't got where I am today by being shy and retiring. So…" He turns to face the twins. "I have a brother and sister?"

"You do." I nod. "Jake and Grace. They're in a band called *Temptress*. They played in the Big Top at Download and gained a manager. Music obviously runs in the family."

"Hi." Jake manages to croak out a greeting. "Cool set at Download."

"Hello Leigh." Grace blushes but carries on. "Great to meet you."

"Cheers." Leigh manages a small smile and then taps his mobile phone. "Hey Jake….Grace …I'm a bit of an arsehole, but tell you what… give me a phone number and I'll see if I can get you a support slot on one of our UK dates coming up."

Jake's phone is in his hand and in front of his brother in record time.

"Wow! Thanks! Here's my number you can copy. Can I have yours?"

Leigh hesitates slightly before turning his phone in Jake's direction.

"Sure."

DI Lambert has been patiently waiting his turn to speak, which he does during the lull in conversation.

"Mr Havilland, I'll need your parents' address in Australia before you go. I don't suppose for a minute they've gone back there, but it'll be somewhere to start."

The heavies move forward as Leigh nods and stands up to leave.

"I'll write it down. They live in a house on my gated estate, but I'm sure they'll be in touch with me sooner or later. This whole scene is unreal, but I guess I'll have to get used to it."

"Yeah, so will we." Gerrie holds out his hand. "We never thought we'd ever see you again."

Leigh shakes Gerrie's hand and turns to me as I speak. I want to wrap my arms around my son, but he is like a stranger to me.

"I hope we can see more of you? As well as a sister and brother, you have grandparents too who are eager to meet you."

Leigh shrugs.

"I'm pretty busy touring, but get some time off at Christmas. Maybe then?"

I nod as I sigh in a kind of desperate hope that my family might have a slim chance of one day becoming complete again.

Chapter Twenty-Eight

My mother is over the moon with joy, and now I cannot help but smile at Eila's beaming face which fills up most of my iPad screen, nudging out Brett who has been surprisingly anxious for updates.

"Sophie, that's wonderful news!"

"It is." I agree while raising a hand to acknowledge Brett. "But … he's like a stranger to us. He's even got a different name … *Leigh Havilland.*"

"Of course he'll be a stranger." Brett's sonorous tones are instantly recognisable as he tries to get a look-in. "What do you expect?"

I sigh.

"Not much, I suppose. He's a famous rock star. He doesn't need us in his life."

Eila waved away my reply.

"You are so wrong! Blood is thicker than water, and you and Gerrie are his *real* parents. One day I hope Leigh will come to Gaborone – maybe even do a concert?"

I give a wry laugh with the absurdity of it.

"I'll tell him his grandmother's asking to see him."

"*And* his grandfather." Brett chuckles. "I'm ready to meet my grandson anytime. Gerrie, how's it going with you?"

Gerrie up until now has been sitting next to me on the settee in silence. I turn to face him, but he's staring down at the floor holding his head in his hands. On hearing his father's voice Gerrie looks up.

"Dad, there's something I've got to tell you. The story will probably come out sooner or later, but it'll ease my conscience if I spill the beans now rather than you hear it from somebody else.

I know what's coming. Brett and Eila look interested and wait for Gerrie to begin speaking, which he does after a short hesitation.

"Mum… Dad…back when Sophie was pregnant for the first time, as you know I had the chance to be what Leigh is now, a famous musician."

I see Brett nodding on the screen and Eila looking expectantly at Gerrie, who continues speaking. I take my husband's hand to offer a silent support.

"The ransom money that you paid – it wasn't for Leigh, and he wasn't kidnapped at first. We handed him over to our friends to hide him for a week in the hope that you'd pay forty five thousand pounds so that I could go on tour with the band and support *Death Throes*, who were as famous then as Leigh is now. Our so-called *friends*… they kept Leigh and took him to Australia. You did come up with the money eventually, but the deadline to pay had gone."

There is an agonising hush while my in-laws digest this information. Eila is the first one to break the silence.

"So… you're saying that Leigh wasn't kidnapped but then he was?"

"Yep, that's about it." Gerrie sighs. "I was so determined to be a rock star, but didn't bank on losing Leigh because of my dream. But I did, didn't I?"

He sounds painfully contrite. I squeeze his fingers and scan the screen for Brett and Eila's response. Brett clears his throat and is the first one to reply.

"We all have regrets, Gerrie. I lost *you* because I wanted you to become something you didn't want to be. As I've grown older I've realised that we cannot control our children when they become adults. We have to let them go their own way. I only wish I'd been less stubborn and had given you the money when you asked for it instead of purposely hanging out until the last minute just to spite you and to try and bring you back home."

This is a revelation indeed. There is a release of pent-up emotion from Gerrie, who hangs his head to disguise falling tears of relief. It's down to me to think of something to say.

"Sorry." I blurt out. "Sorry for everything."

Brett speaks in Afrikaans to Gerrie, who looks up at his father and gives him a smile. They end the call and we sit there without speaking while Gerrie composes himself. When he rubs his eyes and gives me a cuddle I lean against him.

"What did your dad say?"

Gerrie kisses the top of my head.

"It's an old Africaans saying - that the child often looks and acts like the parent. I think what he means in a roundabout way is not to make the same mistakes he did so that we end up losing Leigh altogether. We've got to make an effort to try and bring him into the family."

"Easier said than done." I reply. "We haven't even got his phone number."

Gerrie suddenly lets go of me and gets to his feet.

"But Jake has." He smiles at me as he makes for the door. "Nobody is going to put on my epitaph that I didn't do my best to get to know my son. We've got to get Jake and Leigh talking first, and then hopefully we might be able to have a go."

His father's words are obviously having an impact, but of course I'm still grounded in reality and wonder if we're already too late to catch that particular train. Only time will tell. I follow him up to Jake's room and wonder how on earth we even begin to make friends with a famous rock star.

Mike Prentiss excels himself and gets our story published on the first page of The Daily Trouper, along with *have you seen them* photos of Ace and Maxine. We wait in the hope that somebody somewhere will recognise them.

Chapter Twenty-Nine

True to his word and I expect with a little nudging from Jake, we hear that Leigh has arranged a twenty minute support slot for *Temptress* before his gig with *Ricin* at the Brighton Centre at the end of July. It's one of *Ricin's* smaller venues with just 4,500 seats, and it's perfect for the twins' first big concert experience. Our garden becomes a hive of frantic activity and noise, and we become the neighbours from hell as the band polish their songs to perfection in the garage. Access All Areas passes arrive in the post, and the twins even wear them to bed.

Before the gig our twins turn seventeen. We reluctantly give them what they want and splash out on a course of driving lessons for them, although my heart is in my mouth at the thought of them out there and vulnerable on the road. Gerrie tells me it's time I let them grow up, but what mother wants to think of her children behind the steering wheel of a car at the mercy of every drunk, drugged or speeding driver? They are in their element, particularly Jake, and their driving instructor informs us that Jake will be ready for his test in no time at all.

Leigh phones Jake on the day before the gig to invite me, Gerrie, the twins and Chang and Ricky for an overnight stay at Brighton at his expense and a practice at the actual venue. Luckily the term has ended at college, and Gerrie is able to drive us down to the coast at short notice. The nursery is also in the process of closing for the summer holidays. I make some last minute arrangements with my deputy, and look forward to joining in the general hubbub and excitement.

It's a blazing hot day as we climb into the car for the trip down the A23 to Brighton. The twins have been buzzing all week, and Gerrie and I cannot wait to meet Leigh again, whom we haven't seen since Download. I thank the gods above and Leigh's good sense that *Temptress* has not been invited to support *Ricin* at the last of their UK gigs – Wembley Arena; a venue seating 12,500 people.

As Gerrie starts the engine I check my phone in case there has been any update regarding Ace and Maxine's whereabouts, but there are no new messages. Of course it has occurred to all of us that Leigh might know exactly where they are, and there's also the fact that he might have even bought them a hideaway somewhere. However, if he has done so he certainly hasn't disclosed any information to the police thus far.

Grace is saving her voice and only speaks when necessary. Jake holds Gerrie's prized Flying V and silently practises a solo, but the neck of the guitar I suspect is becoming somewhat of an irritation to his sister.

"Get that thing out of my face!"

Grace is wound up tighter than one of Jake's guitar strings. I look over my shoulder at the two of them.

"Jake ..."

"Sorry Mum." Jake sits sideways in his seat. "How's this?"

Gerrie glances up into the rear view mirror.

"As long as it doesn't poke me in the back of the head."

Peace reigns supreme. I doze a little bit, lulled by Grace's quiet humming to Jake's guitar. When the sea and crowded stony beach come into view, the twins spot the Brighton Centre along the seafront almost at once.

"There it is!" Jake points a finger. "It's got *Ricin's* name on the billboard!"

"Not ours?" Grace chuckles.

Jake slumps back in the seat and taps a number on his mobile phone.

" 'Fraid not, sister."

"Keep at it." Gerrie laughs. "And you'll get there."

We double back and find the venue's car park, whilst Jake chats to Chang and Ricky who are already inside. Thankfully Jake only has Gerrie's guitar to carry, as Leigh had informed him there would be no time on the actual night to set up their own equipment. We feel like VIPs as we place a free car pass on the front of the windscreen, while other holidaymakers queue up at the ticket machine. The twins rush off inside the venue, leaving Gerrie and I to walk in at a more leisurely pace. I hold Gerrie's hand and feel his warmth calming my nerves.

"I wonder where we'll be sleeping tonight?"

"On the beach probably." Gerrie laughs. "Fancy a quick one under the pier?"

We're giggling like two teenagers as we approach the front of the venue, where I recognise Leigh's two heavies from the police station standing on duty just inside the main entrance. One of them opens the glass door for us and ushers us through. I feel awkward when I see Leigh standing at the back of the foyer chatting to the twins and their bandmates.

"What shall we do?" I hiss to Gerrie. "Shall we go up and join them?"

"Sure." Gerrie waves to Leigh. "Why not?"

Leigh beckons us over. I push back memories of our first meeting and prepare to greet my son again, who is wearing khaki shorts, another white vest and flip flops, together with the ubiquitous baseball cap and sunglasses. His long hair is tucked in under the back of his vest.

"Hey." Leigh shakes Gerrie's hand and shoots me a dazzling smile. "How's it going?"

I'm disappointed that he hasn't called us by our names, although I don't expect for a moment that he'll ever call us Mum and Dad. I give him a nod and return his smile.

"Fine thanks. How's you?"

"Chillin'." Leigh performs a quick pirouette. "Been sunbathing on the beach this morning and no-one recognised me in this get-up! I enjoy doing the smaller gigs – they're not so impersonal."

He's relaxed and affable. The twins are looking at their brother as though he is some kind of Adonis. Chang and Ricky are mute.

"When's practise time then?" Gerrie breaks the sudden silence. "Have they got time for lunch?"

Leigh checks the time on his phone.

"Absolutely. I expect there'll be food set up backstage now – it's all part of the rider. Come on - follow me."

He turns around and disappears along one of the side corridors. We bring up the rear and arrive at a door bearing the sign *No members of the public beyond this point.* Leigh waves us through into a small room containing a long wooden table and several chairs. The other members of *Ricin* are already helping themselves to sandwiches, pasta, salad and fruit.

"Get stuck in guys. Steve and Ed, these are *Temptress* who are doing the support slot. Gerrie and Sophie, meet Steve and Ed, otherwise known as *Ear* and *Noise*."

"Pleased to meet you."

Gerrie shakes hands all round and then attacks the food. The twins, Chang and Ricky soon find their feet and recover their voices. I'm pleased that Leigh has introduced us to Steve and Ed, who seem quite different from their on-stage personas. Aussie twang mixes in with South London slang and Gerrie's South African vernacular. We're a very mixed group who sit down for lunch, but within half an hour we're chatting away with no awkward silences. Members of Leigh's staff clear away the plates and bring dessert, and I feel like a queen; well okay, perhaps a princess. No mention is made of Ace and Maxine. I'm not sure if Steve and Ed know that we're Leigh's birth parents, and so I decide to keep quiet on that front.

The hall seems enormous without an audience. Gerrie and I take front row seats next to Leigh. Steve and Ed have gone off in disguise to jet-ski, with instructions from Leigh to return after two hours for *Ricin's* practice. Chang checks out Steve's drum kit and plays a few rolls and paradiddles.

"He's got the hang of it already." Leigh nods in approval. "He'll be fine."

My heart gives a lurch as the small figure of my daughter walks out onto the stage, taps the microphone, and takes a look around her as Jake plugs his guitar into the amplifier. She looks pale and petrified.

Ricky plays a few notes on his bass guitar and then gives the twins a thumbs-up. Chang's sticks count out four beats to a bar, and then the band launch into their first song. Leigh's flip-flops and Gerrie's fingers are tapping out the beat within minutes, and I watch with a delicious happiness as Grace grows more confident with every song.

"They're bloody good!" Leigh sits forward in his seat. "It's not death metal, more melodic metal …but my brother and sister have definitely got talent!"

Gerrie gives him a nudge.

"Of course they've got talent! All three of you have taken after *me*!"

I look at them sitting there like two peas in a pod. I should be happy at this moment in time, but all that's running through my mind is the whereabouts of Ace and Maxine. Leigh doesn't seem too bothered that they're missing, which to me is further evidence that he knows where they really are. I am silently screaming for justice, and I will not rest easy until I see them behind bars.

Chapter Thirty

After *Ricin's* practice we take over the upstairs restaurant, which luckily is not open to the public until the evening of the gig. Staff have moved several tables so that we can all sit together, and at the hatch there's a large vat of mouth-watering chicken, vegetables and dumplings bubbling in stock, and two more containing beef curry and aromatic rice. What with the roadies, drivers and heavies there are 17 of us for dinner, and as the vats slowly empty I am pleased to observe that Leigh is chatting quite easily with Jake and Grace. He's quite polite to Gerrie and me, but I notice a reserve that isn't there when he talks to the twins.

I feel drawn to Leigh's face and several times he catches me staring at him, as I'm still pinching myself that he's really back with us. His mobile phone rings constantly, and although I know he's not stupid enough to chat to Ace or Maxine, the fact that he considers them his parents is enough for me to know that they will always be a part of his life.

Beside me, Gerrie pushes his chair back and stands up.

"I'm going to get another helping of curry. Want some?"

I shake my head.

"I'll wait for dessert."

He moves past the others towards the queue at the serving hatch, and I see Leigh stand up while watching his retreating back. Leigh has finished eating and I assume he's going to stand with Gerrie in the queue, but he comes over towards me and sits down in Gerrie's seat.

"Sophie – can I call you Sophie?"

I'd rather he called me 'Mum', but that's something for the far-distant future, if it ever happens at all. I nod and once again curse the day that Maxine was born.

"Sure. That's my name."

He smiles, but the smile falters on his lips as he begins to speak.

"I know you're my birth mother and all that, but it doesn't change the fact that Mum and Dad brought me up. Without their encouragement I'd still be doing the circuit round Sydney's bars and clubs. I owe it all to them. Know what I mean?"

This stranger is ours, Gerrie's and mine, but somehow he's not; he's Ace's and Maxine's. However, I do know what he means for sure.

"I'm getting the idea."

The blue eyes bore into mine.

"Think about your parents. Would you like to see *them* go to jail?"

I meet his gaze timidly at first, but then with years of contained fury.

"Your grandfather is no longer alive, but neither of them have ever done anything that would warrant a jail term… such as kidnapping a baby."

I'm losing the game here, and he knows it. I'm aware that Gerrie is watching us from the queue.

"Dad has fatty liver cirrhosis, and Mum's having counselling and lots of therapy to deal with past problems - unresolved issues from her childhood and her teenage years. She's a tortured soul, but she's always been there for me and I want her to carry on having the help she needs. Neither of them will ever get any help in jail."

I shrug.

"They should have thought of that before they took my baby."

The ice blue eyes twinkle menacingly.

"You're not getting what I'm on about."

I see Gerrie coming towards us, and he's looking at me inquisitively.

"I know exactly what you want." I hiss. "You want me to drop all charges so that you can bring Ace and Maxine out of wherever you've hidden them."

"In a nutshell, or you'll never see me again if you spill the beans to the police." Leigh stands up. "You're very astute and understand all. One day you may be surprised - my two sets of parents might get along quite famously … with me in the middle. Think about it. You could even move to Australia and live on my estate – there's plenty of room, and you won't have to worry about a thing in your old age because I'm a millionaire several times over."

Then with a wink of his eye he's gone, and Gerrie's back with a second plate of steaming curry and rice.

"*This* memory foam mattress is worth the price of our family suite for a start. I'm glad I'm not paying for it though."

Gerrie snuggles down in bed and watches me in my nightshirt applying aqueous cream to my face. I'm thinking of the twins asleep in their rooms next door, while Leigh, Chang, Ricky and the other members of *Ricin* bed down in the tour bus at the back of the venue. I've enjoyed the day, and know what I must do.

I sigh.

"We've got to talk about something."

Gerrie makes a face.

"What have I done now? Pissed on the toilet seat again?"

Despite my worries I have to chuckle. I brush my hair and get into bed beside him.

"No, it's about Leigh."

I cuddle up to Gerrie's chest and try to stop my brain firing in all directions.

"What about him?"

"He spoke to me while you were queueing up for more food. He knows where Ace and Maxine are. He wants us to drop all charges and for all of us to kiss and make up, otherwise he says we'll never see him again."

"Jesus!" Gerrie props himself up on one elbow and looks at me. "He said that?"

"Yep." I nod. "If we don't do as he says, we'll lose him a second time. I haven't even got to know him properly yet."

Gerrie flops down onto the pillow, looks up at the ceiling and sighs.

"The bastards should pay for what they did."

"Of course they should." I agree. "But we'll lose all contact with Leigh again if they do. He said we could even live on his estate if we wanted to, and we'd never have to worry about a thing in our old age."

Gerrie gives a snort.

"Apart from living next door to the fuckers who kidnapped our son."

"What d'you want to do?" I sit up and put my arms around my knees. "This is tearing me up."

Gerrie sits up and puts an arm around my back.

"Do you want to keep in touch with him then?"

"Of course I do!" I exclaim. "Don't you?"

"Yeah, I do." He nods. "How could anyone *not* want to?"

I feel a sense of relief at last, together with a surprising acceptance.

"Then we have no choice. We'll have to contact DI Lambert and drop the case."

Chapter Thirty-One

From my vantage point in the wings I can see the venue slowly filling up with twentysomething fans wearing black *Ricin Rocks!* tee-shirts, jeans, extensive tattoos, and chains. They look a bit of a dodgy crowd that you wouldn't want to meet in a dark alleyway, and I'm glad Security has allowed Gerrie and me to stand on the side of the stage instead of down in the stalls. The twins have gone off to warm up, and there's nothing to do but let the last few seconds go by and listen to pounding Metallica through the speakers.

"Christ! What a rum old lot!" Gerrie peeps out behind the curtains. "I should have brought my switchblade."

"Don't worry if you haven't got one." I grin at him. "The heavies are probably giving them out at the door."

Gerrie takes a last look from behind the curtain.

"Hope they don't start pissing in bottles and throwing them on the stage."

I take a second glance for flying bottles as the lights dim and Metallica fades to black.

"They take bottle tops away at the bar."

Our twins walk out onto the stage, together with Ricky. Chang takes his seat at the drums, and Grace speaks, quite confidently, into the microphone.

"Hi! We're *Temptress*, and we're here to rock this joint for twenty minutes!"

There is a polite round of applause as Jake strums the first power chords. The sound effect in the wings is different than sitting out front, but I'm sure I'll be able to take some great action side-view shots with my camera when there's a burst of overhead spotlights.

I'm aware that Leigh has come out to stand beside us, making sure he is well hidden behind the safety curtain.

"Well?" He shouts in my ear. "What did you decide?"

I hate to give Ace and Maxine the satisfaction, but there's nothing else I can do.

"We'll ask DI Lambert to drop the case!" I shout back. "So don't worry!"

He nods and appears pleased. I refuse to let Maxine spoil any more of my evening, and I snap away with my camera and enjoy the brief concert. The audience's reaction boosts Grace's confidence, and she appears at ease on the stage, flouncing about in black frills and stiletto boots. Chang and Ricky prove a tight rhythm section, with Jake's guitar solos gaining much applause. The support gig ends up a runaway success, and I see a queue to buy *Temptress* CD's form at the front of the stage after the last song finishes. Jake is kept busy taking money while Ricky and Chang give out the CDs. Grace sits by the monitors and lets her legs swing over the front of the stage, causing every male in the queue to have trouble taking their eyes off her. Gerrie keeps quiet guard from the wings, and when all the CDs are sold they walk off to much greater applause then when they came on.

I keep my place in the wings with Gerrie and Grace to watch

Ricin perform. Jake manages to inveigle himself in the thick of the mosh pit, and there is much thrashing and banging of heads until I begin to worry about his neck muscles. I must admit that death metal isn't really my thing, but I enjoy watching Leigh's expertise at controlling a crowd once again. He's like a different person on stage; aggressive and obviously a born leader, and I feel a pang of regret for his father, who was denied the same chances. I shout in Gerrie's ear during a brief lull between songs.

"Do you feel envious of his life?"

To my surprise he shakes his head.

"I thought I would, but I don't. All I see is the responsibility to keep the tour trucks rolling so he can maintain his lifestyle and pay the wages of all the hangers-on. The whole thing must be a millstone around his neck. Perhaps I wouldn't have thought about that too much when I was his age, but then again I'm older and wiser now."

From what I can see, Leigh seems to be positively thriving, even whilst carrying the proverbial millstone. Gerrie undoubtedly had the motivation in his younger years, but I know that losing the chance to tour and the breakdown after Leigh's disappearance definitely caused a loss of drive and ambition. It's as though he gave up and settled for whatever life could give him. As he struts his stuff in front of thousands, I grudgingly give Ace and Maxine some credit for recognising Leigh's talent and pushing him out there into the limelight.

The audience scream for more at the end of two encores. I look down into the pit of iniquity and see Jake, Chang and Ricky sweating and ecstatic pushed up against the front barrier. Grace thank goodness has stayed with us in the wings, and I feel my eyes tearing up at the love that's pouring out from the crowd. Then to my utter astonishment, Leigh turns towards the three of us and beckons us forward before speaking into the microphone.

"Hey! I've found my birth parents recently, or rather…they found *me*!"

Another cheer goes up that rumbles seemingly forever around the auditorium. Leigh grins and waves us towards him again, laughing at our hesitancy.

"Come out! Come out wherever you are … Gerrie and Sophie!"

I want to die with embarrassment. Gerrie's already walking out onto the stage. Grace laughs and gives me a push. Gerrie looks back and takes my hand, and suddenly I'm standing there in front of over four thousand people.

"Give 'em a cheer!"

The answering roar is deafening. Leigh is in his element, bathed in sweat and full of adrenaline. I hadn't banked on this. One wet arm comes around my neck, and another around Gerrie's. Jake, Chang and Ricky go wild in the front row below, and I suddenly feel like a rock star. It's my five minutes of fame and I take a bow. It may be all I'll ever get, and so I decide to make the most of it.

We're still buzzing as the crowd file out. To go back to the hotel and try to sleep would be impossible. Gerrie, Grace and I move backstage as the roadies come on stage to dismantle the equipment. Sweat-soaked and on a high, Jake, Chang and Ricky run past the security guards to meet us and to congratulate Leigh and the band. Suddenly the backstage rooms are full of people. Members of staff, and few trusted fans wait with a group of scantily clad young women for their chance to speak to Leigh, and reporters from the local tabloids and music magazines swarm around taking pictures. Restaurant staff set up a long table laden with food and drink for a midnight feast. Gerrie and I take a back seat, but Grace, Jake, Chang and Ricky make sure they get their photo in the next day's newspapers.

The hubbub begins to decrease after the press leave around 11.30pm. Leigh and the band return freshly showered, and we get our chance to congratulate our son. Gerrie shakes his hand, and I summon up all my courage and give him a small kiss on the cheek.

"You certainly know how to hold a crowd." I smile at him. "Thanks for calling us up …I think. I didn't know what to do with myself."

"No sweat." Leigh laughs as he tips a bottle of beer down his throat. "It's not every day you find out that you have four parents."

I refrain from reminding him that actually he has two real parents and two imposters, and listen instead as Gerrie interrupts with a question he knows will detract me from my train of thought.

"Where are you off to after this?"

"Up to Manchester and then to Wembley for the final gig before a few more concerts in Europe. After that I'm taking some time off at Christmas in December at my place in Rio." Leigh finishes the bottle of beer and takes another. "You ought to come along and hang out. It's fairly warm there in December – Sophie and Grace will be able to work on their tans – my apartment is almost right on Ipanema beach."

"Sounds great." Gerrie nods. "Can't say we've ever been to Rio."

Leigh gives another laugh.

"Now's your chance! The air fares will be on me, by the way."

I think of our usual Christmas visit to Mum up in Astley Green.

"We usually visit my widowed mother on Boxing Day… your grandmother." I tentatively add. "Without us she'll be on her own."

"Bring her along if she wants to come." Lee nods. "It's about time I met her."

He is soon swallowed up by the pretty young things wearing not too much clothing. I sit there feeling 100 years' old eating chicken drumsticks and rice, while trying to imagine laying on Ipanema beach. I wonder if the failsafe swimming costume I've had for years will suffice or whether I ought to buy a new one.

It's only when we are driving home later that day that we remember our twentieth wedding anniversary; we had both totally forgotten it. Gerrie stops at a florist and buys me a dozen red roses, while Jake and Grace sleep soundly in the back seat.

Chapter Thirty-Two

So much happened during the summer that it's a bit of a let-down to return to the nursery at the start of the autumn term. I immerse myself in my child-centred world, all the time thinking about my eldest son whose childhood was snatched away from us. Gerrie returns to his lecturing duties and the twins to their studies, but I feel a restlessness that wasn't there before; a growing need to get to know Leigh better and to take my place as his rightful mother. My continuing seething anger at Ace and Maxine knows no bounds.

Jake is the first to tentatively forge a contact with his brother on social media, closely followed by Gerrie and Grace. I don't mind using Skype to chat to Eila and Brett, but I've never had any dealings with Facebook and Twitter in the past as I've always considered them a massive time-suck. However, Grace shows me how easy it is to contact Leigh on Facebook, who I see that apart from his fan-based band page also has a private account just for family and close friends. From Grace's account I see a photo of his tanned and beautiful Australian girlfriend Melody Ayres, and that Nancy Havilland is listed as his mother (there doesn't seem to be an account in Robert Havilland's name). I have to swallow a rush of jealousy as I open an account and send Leigh a friend request, but feel a little pang of delight as the request is accepted two days' later.

I decide not to bombard him with private messages, but wait to find out if he comments on any photos I take or on any status I add to my timeline. When the twins play their gig at the O2 Academy I make sure to upload a two minute video, and I'm thrilled when he leaves a comment from Sweden to say how much he enjoyed watching it, and he shares it to his page. To my horror there ensues a 'like' of the video by Nancy Havilland, whom I promptly block so that she cannot see any more of my posts.

It doesn't take long, and soon I am as addicted to Facebook as are the rest of my family. I find I'm checking my phone during work time like a bloody teenager, just to see if Leigh has left a comment on any of my posts. Within a month or so I screw up the courage to send him a private message saying how much we're looking forward to flying out to Rio, and whether we should book our flights or leave it to him. There's a rather impersonal reply a few days' later giving me an email address and asking us to send all our details to his office staff, who will then post us the tickets.

Jake and Grace sign up for *Ricin's* newsletter and follow the band on their website. They show me a list of all the tour dates, and I secretly check where Ear, Noise and Throat are playing when I'm supposed to be updating children's details in the office. Nursery staff come and see me with a query, and discover me listening to *Ricin's* special brand of death metal on YouTube with my eyes fixed on Leigh. I have a feeling that I'm beginning to become a figure of fun to them. However, as it's my own private nursery and the business loan was paid off years ago, there is nobody who can reprimand me.

Malcom Wainwright earns his keep and obtains some paying gigs and band competitions for *Temptress*. Gerrie and I are kept busy most weekends driving the twins about and hauling stage monitors, P.A equipment and amplifiers. They finish second in a big London competition in Covent Garden and have a growing fanbase, but still the prized record deal eludes them. I ache to ask Leigh for more support gigs for them, but my conscience tells me not to push my luck as he's already paying our air fares to Rio.

At the end of November our air tickets fall on the doormat. I look at them, and see that we will be boarding a non-stop British Airways flight from Heathrow on the morning of Friday 22nd December. The timing will work out just fine for all of us, as nursery, college and schools will break up the previous day. Straight away I'm on Facebook to thank Leigh for his generosity, and I receive a reply that his tour has finished and he is taking some time out in Rio with Melody before we all arrive. Another stab of jealousy hits me that I'll not be the centre of his attention, but then again… it occurs to me that I never was anyway. I want to question him as to whether Ace and Maxine will be there, but I assume that considering the events at Download he would not be foolish enough to have all four of us in the same room ever again. If I see Maxine smirking at Leigh again, I really don't know what I'll do.

Two weeks before we leave for Rio one of my deputies asks if I am okay. I know my work life is suffering, as I no longer much care about the nursery. The twins are busy with their lives and so is Gerrie, and none of them seem to notice the change in me. Hate simmers just below the surface, hidden by my impatience to meet up with Leigh again and make up for all the lost years. I think long and hard about selling the nursery, but wonder if I'm just tired and need a break. I start packing my case and dreaming of the day when my eldest son will see Maxine for what she really is, a kidnapper, and instead recognise *me* as his mother.

Chapter Thirty-Three

It's about a 45-minute journey to Heathrow, and we are all

up ready to go at silly o'clock on the morning of 22nd December. It seems strange not to have prepared my usual mince pies and Christmas pudding or made a Dundee cake, and the fridge is almost bare apart from salad cream and pickles as I check around before we leave. We haven't even bothered decorating a tree this year, as by the time we get back Christmas will be over. Mum has decided not to accompany us as she doesn't like flying, and eleven hours in an aeroplane has put her off.

The twins fall back to sleep by the time we hit Croydon and the A23. I yawn and turn towards Gerrie, who switches on the front windscreen demister.

"I hope we haven't left anything important at home."

"We'll soon find out." He replies drily. "I hope the twins have forgotten their bloody phones."

I chuckle.

"No chance of that. I think Jake's been speaking to Leigh quite often actually."

As I speak I cannot stop that stab of jealousy coming to the fore. I begin to wonder how often Leigh talks to Maxine on the phone; so far he hasn't called me once.

"It's a brother thing I expect." Gerrie shrugs. "I looked up to Ray as a kid. See it from his point of view - an only child finding a brother he never knew he had, and both of them musicians. Not even a *brudder from anudder mudder* as they say, but a real one. It's no wonder they're talking a lot."

Despite my misery I grin at the vernacular being spoken in Gerrie's South African accent. Signs for Heathrow appear as we turn onto the M25. I want to fit into Leigh's world just as easily as Jake has, but I don't know what to say to him. How on earth does one begin to form a bond with a son not seen since he was a new-born baby? I do not particularly like death metal music, and apart from *Ricin*, know of no other bands in that genre to talk to him about. Tendrils of hopeless depression begin to claw at my soul, along with the usual burning jealousy.

Heathrow never sleeps. People rush to and fro on their silent missions, waiting for planes to fly them to loved ones near and far. I have a loved one, but the love is only travelling out in one direction. My heart is heavy as I board the Boeing 747 to Galeao.

"Christ – these tickets must have cost him a fortune."

Gerrie looks around the first class cabin appreciatively. Instead of the usual sardine seating, passengers are testing out deep, comfortable looking chairs which some have already converted to beds. Flutes of champagne and glasses of orange juice wait patiently for consumption on our side tables, together with blankets, pillows, and several salty snacks.

"This is the life!" Grace plonks herself down in her seat and lays out flat. "Night night."

This is first class travel at its best, and I for one am going to make the most of it. I make myself comfortable next to Gerrie, then look across the aisle at Jake.

"Does anyone know what's happening at the other end?"

Jake yawns and leans back in his seat.

"Leigh's sending his driver to pick us up. He's got our flight details."

"I'm glad somebody knows." I reply with some irritation. "I'll wake you up when it's lunchtime."

I'm amazed at how long young people can sleep for. The twins slumber on through take off and the noise of four engines powering their way across the Atlantic Ocean. Gerrie's got his headphones on listening to music, but I cannot concentrate on a novel I bought in the departure lounge. The stewardesses are very attentive and I cannot fault the service. I never thought for a moment I'd ever be part of the 'other half', living in the lap of luxury.

Im tired and in need of a shower. It doesn't help that the twins and Gerrie are rested and full of excitement for the rest of the day ahead.

"There's our names!"   Grace points to a blond Aussie outdoor- type man in some kind of uniform. "Come on Mum!"

I trudge behind them wheeling my case and watch Gerrie shaking hands with Leigh's driver, who takes my luggage and gives me a smile.

"Welcome to Brazil."

I notice how he gives Grace a quick second glance, still in her frilly Stevie Nicks phase.

"Miss – shall I take your bag?"

"It's okay."   Grace shakes her head. "I can do it."

A wall of heat that I'm not used to in December greets us as we step outside into the early evening. It's still light, which is nice too. A rather expensive looking limousine is parked on a meter a short distance away. Blondie gives us a wink as he loads our cases into the boot.

"Make yourselves at home in the back. I'm Keith. It's about an hour's drive to Ipanema."

We merge with the traffic on the *Avenue Vinte de Janeiro* and head North West, judging by Gerrie's compass on his iPhone. I make use of the cold flannels in ice, coconut water, and some kind of delicious chocolate truffles. The twins' stuff themselves with truffles while their heads are turning one way and another out of the darkened back windows, but I feel like crawling into bed and sleeping for a week. I'm dozing when Gerrie nudges me. I look blurry eyed at lovelies parading along a pavement next to what seems like miles of golden sand. There's a calm sea, swaying palm trees, and the iconic statue of Christ the Redeemer watching us atop Corcovado Mountain in the background.

"We're here, Soph."

I'm aware of cameras watching us from every angle as Blondie punches in a code and we enter an air-conditioned foyer. There's a concierge on duty, who waves to Blondie.

"Good evening, Sir."

"Alright, mate?" Keith is the epitome of the affable unflappable Australian. "These are friends of Boz – staying for a couple of weeks."

Boz? Friends? I'm his mother for Pete's sake! I smile at the concierge through gritted teeth and we follow Keith along a corridor, who then punches a code into a machine on a door at the end.

"No keys here. Boz would only lose them anyway."

Soft music is playing. We follow Keith like ducklings out through a huge lounge furnished with squashy sofas, a giant TV set, and a large tastefully decorated Christmas tree standing on an expensive looking Persian rug to where my son sits with his immaculate girlfriend on a glass fronted patio overlooking Ipanema beach. I look away from the beauty of the beach and turn to my right when I hear Grace's sharp intake of breath, because there, lounging around a heart-shaped swimming pool in shorts and tee-shirts, are Ace and Maxine.

Chapter Thirty-Four

Leigh jumps up straight away.

"Hi all. Hope you had a good journey?"

I am speechless with rage at the sight of our son's kidnappers. Ace gets to his feet, but Maxine stays in her lounger looking wary. Leigh comes towards us, shakes Gerrie's hand and gives me a kiss on the cheek.

"I mentioned before that I wanted all four of my parents to get along, so I invited you here to put an end to all the bad feeling and celebrate Christmas with us."

Melody comes over to me. She is coiffed and perfumed up to the hilt.

"Hi Sophie. Can I get you a drink?"

"No thanks." I shoot a deadly glare at Maxine. "I think we'll be staying somewhere else."

"Good luck with that then." Keith shrugs and helps himself to a beer from the ice bucket. "You won't get anywhere round here at Christmas."

Leigh bids us to sit down.

"Not only is there nowhere at this time of year, whatever rooms available would be priced through the roof. Come on Sophie, we're all adults now, and it's Christmas – the season of goodwill."

Gerrie, silent up until now, remains standing with eyes blazing.

"Son, you're walking roughshod over your mother's feelings! We were under the impression that Ace and Maxine would not be here!"

Leigh stands straight in front of Gerrie and meets him eye-to-eye.

"I told you, Gerrie, I have four parents now. We've got to forget what happened in the past and move on."

The two of them stare each other out like prize-fighters. I butt in before Gerrie can think of a reply.

"Move on?" I am aghast at my son's effrontery as I point towards Maxine. *"Move on? Those two fucked up our lives!"*

I never swear in front of the twins, and out of the corner of my eye I see Jake staring at me in surprise. Ace and Maxine, silent and protected by blue sparkling water, have positioned themselves very craftily across the other side of the pool. It would be impossible to get to them without being stopped by either Keith, who has circumnavigated the pool to sit next to Ace, or Leigh himself. There is no way I can get to the bloody woman, rip off her head and chuck her into the pool.

"Can I have a shower, please? It's been a tiring day."

I am deflated and close to tears. Melody immediately plays the genial host.

"Of course. Come with me and I'll show you all to your rooms."

Gerrie is the first to turn away from the staring competition. With Melody in front, he follows behind me along a carpeted corridor, with the twins trailing despondently behind. Melody opens four doors and smiles at us.

"There's a double bedroom with an en-suite bathroom, two single rooms, and another bathroom – all yours. Feel free to make yourselves at home. Dinner is at eight o'clock – a barbeque on the patio. Boz is an expert cook."

I want to sink into Gerrie's arms and howl like a baby. I nod appreciatively and with a superhuman effort stop my lips from trembling.

"Thank you, but why do you call him Boz?"

Melody shrugs.

"That's what I've always called him – he likes it."

She retreats back along the corridor. The twins argue about who will use their bathroom first, while I slip inside Gerrie's arms in the privacy of our room and give vent to my misery.

I must have dozed again because Gerrie's nudging me awake.

"Come on, Soph. Have a shower - I've already had one. It's time for dinner in half an hour."

I reluctantly sit up, disorientated.

"I don't want to go back out there."

"We're expected to. We've got to make an effort to get on with them or you won't see Leigh again – he's already told you that."

I sigh.

"I want to stab her with a thousand knives."

Gerrie gives a wry laugh.

"Then you definitely won't see Leigh again because I doubt he'll visit you in jail."

I know he's right, and it's a situation I've got to come to terms with. I look at my husband, so cool about the fact that we've got to share our son with his kidnappers.

"How do you get your head around it all?"

He gives a shrug.

"Just accept things as they are. No use worrying about something that can't be changed."

I rub my eyes and walk over to the sumptuous black marble en-suite bathroom, all the while thinking of ways to get Ace and Maxine out of my life.

The heat of the day has dissipated, and there's a pleasant aroma of frying steaks as the twins, Gerrie and I find our way out onto the patio. I have a quick peep in the other rooms as we walk along the corridor. Everywhere is expensively and tastefully furnished in a kind of modern minimalist fashion. The walls in the lounge are decorated with garish rugs, photos of the band, and quite a few gold discs, while the bedrooms are painted in pastel shades with matching linen adorning queen size beds. Black marble seems to be the preference in what seems to be three other bathrooms.

"Something smells good." Gerrie rubs his hands together. "Steak! My favourite!"

Leigh is barefoot and wears crisply pressed shorts and short-sleeved shirt, with an apron over the top depicting a naked lady.

He turns T-bone steaks expertly with one hand and waves a greeting with the other.

"Grab yourselves a drink from the table here. Dinner won't be long."

Beyond the patio, nightlife in Rio is getting into gear. Car drivers with loud hooters and riders of motorcycles without silencers compete for the attention of the young and beautiful, who parade along a walkway next to the beach. Gerrie pours cokes for Grace and I, and says nothing as Jake takes a beer. Melody tosses salad and lays out nibbles and plates on a makeshift dining table. She smiles at me nervously as I purposely walk around to the other side of the pool where Ace and Maxine sit sipping cocktails and discretely following my every move. Keith quickly positions himself in-between Maxine and I. I notice Maxine's hair is somewhat redder than it was before as I seat myself on a lounger and decide that being polite is for the weak.

"That coat of paint isn't quite the right colour."

Maxine, obviously rattled, throws me a kind of smile which actually seems more like a grimace.

"Cough up that fur ball, darling, and you'll feel much better."

Gerrie is next to me in an instant. The twins sit silently watching by the side of the pool whilst dipping their toes in the water. Keith flexes his muscles. Ace looks as though he wants to be somewhere else, and Leigh carries on turning steaks.

"Come and get some starters!" Melody calls from the across the patio. "It's all ready!"

Maxine is on her feet first. The devil is in me as she sashays towards us along the tiled surround of the swimming pool, head held high. Before Gerrie or Keith can stop me I leap to my feet, sprint towards her in two steps, and push her sideways into the deep end of the pool. There is a wonderful moment of satisfaction watching her expensive-looking top get ruined in the chlorinated water, before I hear her shout.

"I can't swim!"

Chapter Thirty-Five

Maxine flounders about on the water, coughing and spluttering before disappearing underneath. Ace jumps up and there's a clatter as Leigh's tongs fall on the ground, but in a trice Gerrie has already dived in fully clothed. He pulls her to the side and she clings to the rail, shivering with fright. Ace and Leigh run over to Maxine, each holding out a hand, and my eyes burn her with hatred as they pull her to safety. Dignity gone, she collapses on a lounger, sobbing. Gerrie hauls himself out, looks at me and shakes his head.

"Sophie, this has got to stop!"

Leigh exhales with force as he waggles a finger at me.

"Any more stunts like that and you're going straight back on the next plane!"

I had no idea that Maxine couldn't swim, but right at that moment I don't care. What worries me most is the venom in Leigh's eyes. I realise right then and there that wanting to kill the woman who had brought him up is never going to endear me to him.

"Sorry." I sigh. "It won't happen again."

Maxine sniffs and wipes the water from her face, before waving away my apology.

"I think I deserved it actually. If I were in your shoes I'd probably have done the same."

This is not the reply I am expecting. Leigh, without another glance at me, checks that Maxine is okay before returning to his steaks. Ace sits back down and Gerrie, panting and dripping, pushes past me in a huff.

"I'm going to get changed. You try that one again and I'll put you on the bloody plane myself!"

It occurs to me suddenly that the twins have witnessed everything, and feeling ashamed, I want the patio to open up and swallow me whole. I sink down silently onto a lounger and bury my head in my hands. A motor bike roars past and there is much shouting and what I imagine to be cursing in Portuguese from a crowd of young women on the pavement outside. Time appears to stand still for a moment as nobody speaks. Finally Grace comes over to give me a cuddle and Maxine walks away, announcing that she will return when she has dried off. Ace follows behind her.

Melody announces that the food is ready. Keith fills a plate and disappears inside, as Leigh puts another rack of steaks on the dining table and Gerrie reappears in shorts and a vest, but still with wet hair. He looks at Jake still sitting, rather morosely now, on the tiled surround of the pool.

"Come on Jake, let's get stuck in."

Apart from Grace, everybody is ignoring me. I heave myself up from the lounger, contrite and weary, and walk over to the dining table together with Grace. I hold up both hands in supplication as I approach Leigh.

"I need to apologise. Let's just say that twenty years of pent-up emotion came out all at once."

Leigh takes a huge steak and puts it on his plate. His mouth smiles as he sits down, but his eyes do not.

"Mum seems to want to forget it."

I take a smaller sized steak and some salad, and Grace and I seat ourselves at the table.

"You're very generous, not only in paying our air fares and letting us stay here, but also because you haven't chucked me out tonight. I realised as soon as Maxine went into the pool that I've got to let bygones be bygones."

"It's hard, I know." Leigh nodded. "But hate won't get you anywhere."

"You're very astute for somebody who's not yet twenty." I remark with genuine feeling while spearing a forkful of steak. "How come?"

Leigh looks at Melody, who gazes back at him in adoration.

"My lovely girlfriend here. She's following the Dalai Lama's teachings since she read *The Book of Joy*. Have you read it? I read it to see why she keeps going on about it, and it's true – we have to forgive our enemies. It works. We forgive, but we don't forget. If we don't do that that we're crippled with hate for the rest of our lives."

"Perhaps I need to read it." I make a face. "So sorry."

Melody sits down beside me and gives me a cuddle. I want to cry.

"Forget the past." She smiles at me. "And then you'll get to enjoy time with your long lost son."

Maxine, clad in a white sundress, reappears with Ace. They sit down at the table, followed by Gerrie and Jake. There's an awkward silence, but my eldest son soon finds a way to fill it.

"Eat and enjoy." Leigh helps himself to potato salad. "If you like we can go up Corcovado Hill tomorrow. There's a funicular railway – you don't have to climb it."

"Okay." I laugh. "Sounds good."

I am so grateful to sink into a comfortable bed at the end of what has been a very long day. I wriggle over to Gerrie.

"Are you speaking to me yet? You've hardly said a word to me all evening."

I hear a sigh in the darkness.

"Whatever were you thinking of? You could have killed her!"

"I didn't know she couldn't bloody well swim, did I?" I reply abruptly. "You know how I've felt about Maxine for a long time. I just couldn't help it. It was something that had to be done. Even *she* said she deserved it."

"Sophie, you've got to promise me that nothing like that will ever happen again."

I turn over away from Gerrie, annoyed how he won't let the matter drop.

"I've already said so, haven't I? I was even *talking* to Maxine later on after dinner. Give me a break, for Christ's sake!"

"I know you too well." Gerrie turns his back to me. "You're probably still letting everything fester in your mind."

I am amazed at his powers of perception. Yes, he does know me a bit too well. As I close my eyes I realise that's exactly what I'm doing.

Chapter Thirty-Six

The brooding, ever-watchful figure of Christ the Redeemer

gazes down upon us as we queue with crowds of tourists for train tickets to ride the funicular railway to the top of Corcovado Hill. It's hot as the stationary train waits for stragglers, and I'm already sweating when a band of what I suppose can be called wandering minstrels climb aboard. I know they're only after money, but as the train moves off they are very entertaining and sing well known songs and Christmas carols before passing round the hat and moving on to the next carriage. Gerrie, the twins, Leigh and Melody all sing along too, but I feel rather self-conscious and stay quiet.

Ace and Maxine have decided to stay at the apartment today to give us some time alone with our son, and to my mind that's the least they can do. I watch Leigh, in his usual disguise of baseball cap and sunglasses, as he chats to Jake in the seat in front about band stuff. I feel so happy that our family is complete again. Melody, whom I first assumed was a total air-head, talks to me about Buddhism as the train slowly ascends Corcovado Hill.

"So you go through all these incarnations and learn what it is you need to learn until you eventually find pure spiritual Nirvana, so to speak."

I try and feign some sort of interest, but in reality just want to feast my eyes on the back of Leigh's head.

"Oh."

"Yeah, so you're Sophie in this incarnation, and you've learned to forgive Maxine, or Nancy as we call her, because everyone's happier and you find peace that way."

I wish Melody would shut up.

"Cool."

The train rattles along and I look idly out of the window. We pass homes and gardens set on the hillside, where leathery-skinned locals wave to us as we pass. There's a cooling breeze from the open windows. Grace is immersed in sending a text, and Gerrie, still quieter than usual towards me, sits across the aisle from the boys and joins in with their conversation. Melody's conversation has made me curious about one thing.

"So, do you believe in God, then?"

Melody smiles and shakes her head.

"Not really – it's all about your actions and what you learn on the way to your own personal spiritual Nirvana: Peace, love, understanding, tolerance, forgiveness… that's what I believe in."

"Not chucking somebody who can't swim into a six foot pool of water."

I can see Melody is trying very hard not to laugh.

"Yeah, that's about it."

The train comes to a halt at the top of the hill, and there is a scramble for the lift that bypasses hundreds of steps up past the café with a view. It's too hot for me to even think about climbing, and so Grace, Melody and I wait for the lift while the boys climb the steps.

Coming out of the lift the statue of Christ is huge and forbidding. There's a few more steps to the summit, where a tiny church sits all on its own. An elderly woman is seated just inside the door, who looks us up and down as we enter. The boys arrive sweating and puffing, and are grateful to sit for a moment inside the church. A young man approaches Leigh as he flops down in one of the pews.

"Are you *Throat* from *Ricin*?"

"No." Leigh whispers, "I just look like him."

The youth goes away, taking a second glance.

The café with a view has just one table left for the six of us.

I am glad of a parasol spreading out its arms to give us a modicum of shade.

"Beer for me." Leigh has a quick perusal over the menu. "What about you guys?"

Jake looks at me and tries his luck.

"I'll have a beer."

"Will you?" I shoot him an evil eye. "Is that so?"

"He's nearly eighteen, Soph." Gerrie gives Jake a wink. "Let the leash out a bit."

Leigh chuckles.

"It's not enforced too much here. Nobody will notice."

I point up at the statue.

"*He* will."

"Oh *Mum*." Jake complains. "I'm not going to be legless on one beer."

Grace puts down her menu and looks at me.

"If *he's* having a beer, can I have one?"

I shrug.

"What goes for one goes for the other, but you won't like the taste of it."

"I remember my first taste of the neck oil." Leigh smiles at the memory. "I was fifteen and went to a mate's birthday party. I hated the taste but kept drinking it and got as pi…er… drunk as a skunk. Mum and Dad went ballistic."

Melody touches Leigh's arm and speaks in a quiet voice, causing everyone at the table to strain their ears to listen.

"Boz, don't forget what Rob said, to call them Nancy and Rob while Sophie and Gerrie are staying with us."

Leigh looks up at us as if a light bulb has been switched on inside his head.

"Oh, er…yeah. Sorry. Dad, I mean Rob, suggested this when I talked to him this morning. He's busting his pooper to try and make things right."

The Australian slang makes me smile as I make eye contact with my son.

"Busting his pooper?"

"You know…" Leigh throws me an answering grin. "Going flat out to please. He needs trouble like a third armpit."

The mental image of Ace with three armpits causes me to throw back my head and laugh. Gerrie grins maniacally, and suddenly we're all giggling as the waitress comes to take our order. It seems as though Christ the Redeemer has gazed down upon us and given us all a bit of a reprieve. It feels good.

Chapter Thirty-Seven

It occurs to me that with all the excitement over travelling to Brazil I've totally forgotten to buy any Christmas presents. I discover that Gerrie and the twins have the same problem, and so later on that evening as we saunter out onto the patio after dinner I throw out a question in Leigh and Melody's direction, purposely ignoring Maxine and Ace.

"Where can we go Christmas shopping tomorrow?"

Keith interrupts as Leigh gives him a nod.

"If you like I'll take you to the Barra Mall. You can get anything you want there."

Leigh looks over at Maxine.

"Nancy, Rob, do you want to go?"

I send out a wave of negative vibes.

"I'll leave it, thanks." Maxine shakes her head.

"Yeah, I'll go." Ace tries to mask his nervousness. "I need to get something for Melody. We can get what we want and then find a bar and leave the girls to it, eh Gerrie?"

I hear Gerrie give soft sigh before replying, but am not sure whether it's from relief or disapproval.

"Sure, why not?"

He doesn't look too pleased at the prospect of being holed up in a bar with Ace, but I know he's making an effort for Leigh's sake. Melody puts some ice in a glass and gives us a wave.

"What can I get you guys to drink?"

"Beer please?" Asks Jake hopefully while giving me quick glance.

"Just the one." I give Melody the thumbs up. "And a coke for me please."

"Whatever Jake's having." Grace smiles at Melody. "While Mum's in a good mood."

Gerrie seats himself down across from Ace and Maxine.

"Beer please Melody. You guys missed a great day out today."

Maxine regards me warily as I pull out a chair.

"We went to the beach."

I make a huge effort to maintain *entente cordiale*.

"Seems strange to be swimming in the sea at Christmas."

Maxine's mouth tries hard to break into a smile, but fails.

"Not if you live in Australia."

"So when did you first go there?" Gerrie nods his thanks as Melody hands him a drink. "How did you manage to stay undetected for so long?"

Ace clears his throat and doesn't quite meet our eyes.

"I worked with a gamekeeper learning how to manage the grouse on a farm in the Outer Hebrides first of all. I had a mate who had moved up there who got me the job. The farmer and his wife had no TV and only bought local newspapers. It suited us. We lived in a cottage on the estate for about a year and Maxine helped the farmer's wife when she could, all the while we were sorting out the paperwork and visas for Australia. We used our own passports as we knew you didn't know my real name, which *is* actually Robert Havilland. We didn't need a passport for the baby at that time. Whether or not you knew Maxine's surname we didn't know, so we got married and she became Nancy Maxine Havilland. Her middle name is Maxine, and so she started using *Nancy*, her real Christian name."

"Which I hate, by the way." Maxine grimaces.

I cannot help my reply.

"I suppose you have to make adjustments in life if you decide to be criminals."

"Ouch." Ace pulls a face. "That hurts."

"Can we swim in the pool?" Grace looks at Leigh for approval. "I'm too hot."

Leigh nods his approval and the twins go off to change. Meanwhile I'm all ears to discover the kind of childhood that our son had experienced.

"Leigh was a toddler then, when you went to Australia?"

"Yeah." Maxine nods. "He loved the outdoor life. He learned to swim at three years old. He was singing and playing guitar in bands by thirteen. We knew he was musically talented, and we encouraged it. Actually… I've made a photo album for you that shows nearly every year of his life, as a kind of peace offering. I know you won't accept a Christmas present from us, but I hope you'll take the album if I go and get it from my case?"

Leigh looks at me, waiting for my answer.

"Of course." I nod. "What else is there to say?"

Maxine stands up and moves past me towards the lounge, brushing past the twins who run and jump into the pool. I want to push her into the water again, but I know Jake will make sure she doesn't lose any more of her nine lives. My eyes are stuck on the large red photo album she carries under her arm when she returns.

"Here you are. I'm sorry, but it's all I can give you."

My fingers tremble as I take the only evidence I'll ever have of my son's lost childhood. Gerrie hovers over my shoulder and Maxine looks on as I open the first page to see a well-fed baby with a tuft of light brown hair who is wearing a romper suit and appears to be about five months in age. He lays on his front on a kind of home-made multi-coloured rug. He's smiling and dribbling into the rug.

"We still lived in the farm cottage then. I learned how to make rugs from scrap materials; used to sell them at fairs. Leigh used to pull all the rag bits out if you left him on there long enough."

I touch my baby's face, but alas, the soft skin I remember from all those years ago is but a glossy photo stuck to a piece of card. I can feel my eyes filling with water, and so I turn the page. Standing on two sturdy-looking legs is a barefooted toddler wearing a tee-shirt and dungarees as he squints into the sun. His hat is slanted at an angle, and he holds out one chubby hand towards the camera.

"We'd just settled in Sydney here. He wanted the camera." Maxine chuckles.

The twins race each other up and down the pool as Leigh moves to sit next to me.

"She wouldn't let me have it."

I give a shaky sigh and focus on a grumpy Gerrie clone aged about four. He's wearing a miniature suit and tie with a carnation in his lapel. Maxine peers down at the photo.

"I had a friend who wanted Leigh to be a page boy at her wedding. As you can tell from the photo, he wasn't too keen on getting dressed up."

"I look like a bloody drongo." Leigh laughs.

Ace comes over to stand by Maxine. I look up and see Keith asleep on one of the loungers. Jake dives into the deep end, and I am lost in time.

The next picture shows Leigh in grey shorts, a little white shirt, a blue and red school tie, and a blazer.

"First day at primary school." Ace comments. "He was six there."

"I hated school." Leigh grimaces. "I only went because I loved Jennifer Westley."

"No change there, Boz." Melody rolls her eyes. "Had an eye for the girls even then."

"Was he a good student?" I look up at Maxine. "What subjects did he like?"

"Music, Music, Music and girls." Maxine laughs. "Sometimes girls and then the music."

I cannot help but laugh. Above me I can hear Gerrie chuckling before he speaks.

"A bit like me, then."

"Obviously like father like son." Ace nods. "Genes will out in the end."

I want to hold out my arms to the eight year old boy with sun-bleached hair who is wearing shorts and a tee-shirt, who grasps a fishing rod and sits next to Ace on a large boat.

"I remember that day." Leigh peers at the photo. "We were at the Great Barrier Reef and Rob caught a black marlin. I didn't catch anything."

"Yeah, bloody big thing it was." Ace nods. "I got sunburnt as well."

I wipe away a few stray tears. Leigh squeezes my shoulder.

"A river of tears isn't going to bring your first-born baby back to you, because I'm all grown up. They looked after me well and I never wanted for a thing. I had a great childhood and no complaints, but I never knew Rob and Nancy weren't my real parents."

"I know." I sigh. "If I hadn't seen you at Download you'd still be none the wiser. It's just that you looked so much like Gerrie did at the same age, I *knew* it had to be you." I look over at Maxine. "How did you and Ace get away after Download, by the way?"

Maxine gives a quick glance in Leigh's direction. Leigh I think even manages to look rather sheepish.

"I know a lot of people – people who can give you anything you want, for a price of course."

Grace gets out of the pool and dripping, comes over to look at the album as Maxine's voice drops to a whisper.

"You'll never understand the desperation a woman feels who has been told she'll never have children. I still have counselling back in Oz."

I know I will never be able to pardon or feel sorry for somebody who kidnapped my baby, but I *do* understand, in a grudging sort of way, the turmoil that must have been in Maxine's mind at the time.

I turn over another page of the album. Leigh is standing there in torn jeans and a black tee-shirt, holding a guitar.

"I was eleven then." Leigh points to the picture of himself. "It was my first Stratocaster. Rob and Nancy paid for lessons every Saturday morning for me. Rob showed me the basic chord structures, but Lennie Newton taught me how to do the solos and make it cry. I never looked back."

There is no other photo in the album where Leigh is not holding a guitar or singing into a microphone. I notice his hair becomes longer as the audience grows bigger. Our son's life is told through the pages of the photo album I'll cherish until the end of my days, and Gerrie and I have missed it all. We have a lot to catch up on.

"Thanks Maxine." I hold the album close to my chest. "It's something, at least."

"I'm so sorry." Maxine takes my hand. "So very sorry, Sophie."

There is a moment's silence as though we are all part of a freeze-frame. Jake hauls himself out of the pool and pads over to us. A splash of water falls onto the cover of the album. I let go of Maxine's hand and quickly wipe it away.

Epilogue

$\mathcal{I}$ suppose what can only be described as a truce has settled

on us as we approach the white fronted church of *Nossa Senhora da Misericórdia* for the English-speaking Midnight Mass service on Christmas Eve. Ace and Maxine walk in front, followed by Leigh and Melody, with Gerrie and I and the twins bringing up the rear. A few people recognise Leigh without his hat and sunglasses and I can see them staring, but as we ascend the few steps to the church they melt away and give him the privacy he craves.

I take a seat at the end of a pew next to Gerrie and look down the centre aisle towards the rear wall above the altar, where Christ hangs forlornly on a cross surrounded by gilded pillars to the left and right, which reach up to a decorated and vaulted roof. A kind of peacefulness settles upon me. Right there and then I make amends to a God I've had no time for during the previous twenty years.

Our son is back in our lives and he has been given the best of care by his kidnappers, who just so happen to be seated right next to Gerrie. Over time I must come to terms with the fact that Leigh has been raised rather well by two people I have hated for a very long time. The hate that has been ingrained in my soul must now be changed into something akin to tolerance. It will take me some time to accomplish this, but with every day I hope it will become easier.

I cannot turn back the clock, and so I must learn to be grateful for the coming years in which Leigh, in his wisdom, has promised that all four of his parents will be treated equally. He and Melody will be based in Rio in-between tours, and so Ace, Maxine, Gerrie and I will be able to fly out and stay at his apartment whenever we are free to do so. He still has time to get to know the three grandparents he has never seen, and in the years ahead can forge a greater bond with his younger siblings; perhaps even give *Temptress* some more support gigs. Who knows, in years to come there may even be three rock stars in the family.

In the pew in front of us, the aforementioned younger siblings are looking down at their phones. I give them a nudge as the priest processes down the aisle followed by the choir and a lone choirboy singing the first verse of 'Once in Royal David's City'. His voice is ethereal and pure. It makes me wonder whether Leigh had ever been a choirboy. I make a mental note to ask Maxine when we get back to the apartment.

The End

Other Books By Stevie Turner

THE PILATES CLASS
A HOUSE WITHOUT WINDOWS
FOR THE SAKE OF A CHILD
LILY: A SHORT STORY
NO SEX PLEASE, I'M MENOPAUSAL!
A RATHER UNUSUAL ROMANCE
THE DAUGHTER-IN-LAW SYNDROME
REVENGE
THE NOISE EFFECT
CRUISING DANGER
THE DONOR
REPENT AT LEISURE
LIFE: 18 SHORT STORIES
ALYS IN HUNGERLAND
MIND GAMES
LEG-LESS AND CHALAZA

About The Author

Stevie Turner writes suspense, women's fiction, and darkly humorous novels. She won a New Apple Book Award in 2014 and a Readers' Favorite Gold Award in 2015 for 'A House Without Windows', and one of her short stories, 'Checking Out', was published in the Creative Writing Institute's 2016 anthology 'Explain!' Her psychological thriller 'Repent at Leisure' won third place in the 2016 Drunken Druid Book Award contest.

Stevie lives in East Anglia, UK, and is married with two sons and four grandchildren. She has also branched out into the world of audio books, screenplays, and translations. Most of her novels are now available as audio books, and one screenplay, 'For the Sake of a Child', won a silver award in the Spring 2017 Depth of Field International Film Festival. 'A House Without Windows' gained the attention of a New York media production company in December 2017. Some of Stevie's books have been translated into German, Spanish, and Italian.

Social Links

Website:
http://www.stevie-turner-author.co.uk/

Facebook:

https://www.facebook.com/StevieTurnerAuthor/

Twitter:

http://www.twitter.com/StevieTurner6

Goodreads:

https://www.goodreads.com/author/show/7172051.Stevie_Turn
er

If you have enjoyed this book, please consider leaving a review.

You may also like *The Donor*, another family drama also by Stevie Turner.

www.ingramcontent.com/pod-product-compliance
Lightning Source LLC
Chambersburg PA
CBHW070636170726
48291CB00003B/1034